THE NARROWS

NENE DAVIES

ALSO BY NENE DAVIES

The Distance Series

"If you like everything a good story has to offer - love, loss, drama, suspense, loyalty, betrayal - you'll like Nene Davies' contemporary fiction Distance Series."

K.A. HOUGH

Distance

Goodreads Listopia - The Aussie List. No. 3

Queensland Fiction - No. 10

"A frank and intimate tale of new beginnings."

THAT BOOK YOU LIKE

Further

"If you have read Distance and enjoyed it, you will love Further. There is the same mix of drama, laughter, angst and sadness but overall the importance of family is the main theme."

GREAT AUSSIE READS

Surfacing

"Nene Davies takes the reader on quite a journey with well drawn characters and vivid descriptive prose that draws you right in to the story."

GREAT AUSSIE READS

ISBN: 978-0-6482951-2-9

First published in Australia by Hammer and Tongs Publishing, 2020

Printed by Caidex Communications

For W.G.

Barren. What a word.

ONE

THE NARROWS - SURREY ENGLAND

1965

K aren Douglas loved telling people her address. Loved her brand new kitchen and her husband's garage at their detached house in the stockbroker belt. She liked living in the Home Counties in a cul-de-sac within walking distance of the train station. *The Narrows* had a nice ring to it. She liked going up to town for a night out, or a day's shopping. She liked the money Eric earned and the fast lifestyle it brought; the parties and balls, company drinks and lunches aboard the boss's yacht moored on the East coast, the clothes and makeup, the shoes and beaded evening bags.

Karen adored it all and detested it all at the same time, for what was this life, and a house in a sought-after area and money in the bank and a handsome husband worth without a child to complete the picture?

Karen didn't know what she'd do, if not for Vera. Sisters-in-law who were also best friends and lived just a few doors down from each other. A housewife like Karen, with an urbane, charming husband like Karen's, a kitchen filled with the latest gadgets like Karen and a wardrobe and bank balance to match. There was just one difference - Vera had children. Children, plural whereas Karen couldn't even have one.

It could have made Karen hate Vera, but it didn't. It could have made Karen hate her nephews, but it didn't. The only person Karen hated, was herself. *A born mother*, her own mum used to say. *You're a born mother*. Well, apparently not.

And it wasn't for the want of trying. Karen was desperate for a child, but Mother Nature had other plans. No babies for her.

A NEW CLIENT was in town. A big, important, cashed-up *American* client. Eric and Edward were abuzz.

Karen and Vera were off to London to buy dresses for dinner. Dinner in a fancy club on Friday night with their husbands, the American client and his wife, plus the big boss.

Monday morning saw Karen checking her reflection in the mirror before leaving the house. She liked how the geometric pattern of her shift dress worked so well with bright tights and low block heels. Small and slight, her pixie-cut accentuated her youthful face and she knew she looked good. Vera was more of your beehive and mini-skirt variety. Very mod. Very cool.

The women were to catch the 9.00am train and be back by

3.00pm, for when Vera's twins Mark and Paul would be home from school. It was a bitter pill for Karen, to organise her entire day around Vera's children, but she was used to it. It was the price she paid - one of many, many costs.

They walked together to the train station, bought return tickets to Waterloo and waited on the platform, which earlier that morning had been home to dozens of bowler-hatted, umbrella-wielding city gents, and women in cats-eyes glasses and neat suits, all heading into London to earn their daily crust. Karen thought back to the time before she was married, when she too worked in the city. Flat-sharing with a couple of girls from college; an exciting time of independence and having her own money. Saturday afternoons spent browsing boutiques on Carnaby Street, experimenting with make-up, buying records from the Top Ten, flirting with fashion and boys and getting the giggles at the pictures and having the usherette shush them.

And then one day noticing Eric at work; young, good looking, creative and cool, as she sat there, bashing out page after page in the typing pool.

Eric wore tailor-made suits and listened to modern jazz. He claimed to have a Lambretta, a red one he said and she'd listened with wide-open eyes until the weekend trips to Brighton on the back of his scooter didn't eventuate and Karen realised he was as nervous and naive as she. Five years ago, they'd made a cute couple.

THE DINNER WAS at a club in Mayfair that Karen had never been to before and the two couples planned to travel up to town by taxi, buoyed by a few drinks at Vera and Edward's beforehand. Edward was keen to show off their new cocktail cabinet.

'Oh it's lovely, Ed.' Karen ran her hand over the smooth wooden top.

'Ta da!' Edward opened the curved double doors with a flourish. 'Whatcha fancy? You're a Babycham girl aren't you?'

Karen laughed lightly. 'Sometimes, but I'll have a gin and tonic if you've got one please.'

Edward squatted in front of the cabinet and moved bottles aside. 'Vera?' He said, over his shoulder. 'Bacardi and Coke?'

His wife glanced up from her spot on the sofa, where she was sitting with Eric. 'You know it!'

Edward fished about in the cabinet again and retrieved the spirits and mixers, then made a great show of removing sliced lemons from a covered dish on top of the cabinet and pulling the lid off a red ice bucket. A matching soda syphon sat alongside.

Karen wandered away as he prepared the drinks and went to sit on one of the two armchairs facing the sofa.

'Boys in bed?' she said to Vera with a glance at the ceiling.

Vera nodded. 'Anna's reading them a story.'

'She's so good with them, isn't she? And only a young thing herself.' Karen took her gin and tonic from Edward, with a smile.

Vera accepted her drink too. 'She'll be eighteen at Christmas,' she added.

'No!'

'Yup. Next thing I know she'll be leaving school, getting a job and not wanting her babysitting pocket money any more.'

'Oh you'll miss her.'

'Definitely. It's hard to find someone you can trust and Anna's such a good girl. I don't know what we'll do.'

Karen felt a twinge of pain. She'd have taken Vera's babysitter worries in a heartbeat if she only had children who needed one.

'Beer, Eric?' said Edward in the pause that followed.

Vera picked up her satin clutch bag and removed a pack of smokes. 'Light me up, someone,' she said and waved the cigarette in front of her face.

All four sat in companionable silence for a few moments and then Vera stubbed out her cigarette in the ashtray on the coffee table.

'Tell us about this client. Do we have to be on our best behaviour?' She winked at Karen.

Edward grinned. 'He's a big friendly fella with a wallet the size of Texas. Lovely bloke, actually. It'd be great to get this account.'

Karen tilted her head back and blew smoke towards the ceiling. 'What's he selling?'

'Ciggies.'

'For real? What's his company?'

'Hasting.'

'Hasting what?' Karen shifted slightly.

'Just Hasting. It's the family name,' said Edward.

'Hasting Cigarettes,' said Karen thoughtfully. 'What do you think of when you hear the word Hasting? Or Hasting's.'

'Battles,' said Vera firmly.

There was a ripple of laughter.

'Yeah,' said Karen, 'or the seaside? Or... you could break it up. Haste...taste...hasty...I don't know...there'd be a way to make it cool.'

'Speaking of,' interjected Ed, 'they're thinking of bringing out a menthol version down the track, too.'

Vera wrinkled her nose. 'Ugh. What's the point?'

'Interesting,' murmured Karen, her forehead creased with concentration.

'It's alright girls,' soothed Eric, 'we're not working on the ad tonight. Hell, we haven't even got the account yet.'

Karen faced him squarely. 'Any minute now, you'll tell us not to worry our pretty little heads about it. I think I'd be good at what you do actually, and let's face it, there's not much for me at home.'

Eric put out his cigarette. The amber glass receptacle was stained with old ash.

There was a slightly heavier pause than earlier.

Edward got to his feet. 'Another?' He held out his hand to take Karen's glass.

IT WAS TOO crowded in the back of the cab for Karen's liking. She and Vera sat next to one another while their husbands perched 'like elephants on a razor blade,' according to Vera, on the fold-down seats facing them. Vera's knees were touching Eric's, but there really wasn't anything they could do about it. The brothers hung on manfully as the vehicle ducked and dived around corners.

'You should've sat on this side,' said Karen to the men as they took another sharp bend, causing Eric to grab Ed's elbow for balance.

'No thanks!' retorted Vera, 'I'm not sitting over there, I feel sick travelling backwards.'

Karen stared out of the window, wondering why she so often felt like the odd one out. Eric and Edward shared the same moody good looks, had many of the same skills and interests and could read one another's minds. Bonded together, they cut a dashing image; two fit, young creatives, making waves in the cutthroat world of advertising. Double Trouble, The Dynamic Duo. For all their similarities though, Karen had always felt life came a little bit easier to Ed. She didn't resent anything, apart from the fact of him having two children, and that feeling of deep-down gut-twisting envy was something she battled with every day. Ed was generous and passionate, completely smitten with his gorgeous wife, and a lovely dad.

And Vera. Just fabulous in every way. Hilarious company, outspoken and strong in a world where women's opinions were often overlooked. Kind too and an absolute rock to Karen. When Vera's own twins, Mark and Paul were born, she'd never let her pride in having produced two healthy babies come before her concern for Karen. She knew how deeply it had bitten. Edward confided to Eric that Vera felt guilty and so, so sad for her sister-in-law. And Karen's sorrow had swelled, but this time compounded by gratitude and love. She was drowning in envy, but could never be bitter and jealous.

'Hey,' murmured Vera now to Karen, 'you look fantastic tonight. Your outfit is so you.'

Karen turned from the window.

'Seriously,' added Vera, 'what did the shop girl call it - space-age spangles? I mean, who else is gonna turn up in a metallic dress? You look a million pounds.'

Karen blinked; her enormous false eyelashes batting up and down like fans. 'Aww thanks. You look amazing, too.' She cocked her head across to Edward. 'Did hubby approve?'

Vera crossed her long slim legs and Karen couldn't help but notice the brothers turn their heads in a concerted effort not to stare.

'Mmm,' said Vera with a cheeky grin, 'and didn't even blink at the price.' Her bronze brocade mini-dress screamed *expensive*. 'Let's get tanked tonight,' she said and they burst out laughing.

TWO

Larry Hasting was a big man. Expansive, affable and loaded with cash.

'Hello, hello!' He held out a giant paw to each of the ladies in turn. 'Larry. Nice to meet you.'

'Hello,' said Karen and then to the woman sitting next to him. 'Barbara? Hello, I'm Eric's wife, Karen.'

'Hi,' said the woman and smiled from under her blonde fringe. The sequins on the cuff of her white dress sparkled in the light.

'Hello,' said Vera warmly and shook hands. She nodded to a man seated the other side of Barbara. 'William.'

William Shepherd, Eric and Ed's boss planted a kiss on her cheek. 'Looking lovely Vera, as always. Evening, Karen. Yes, lovely. Well let's get a round of drinks in.' He summoned a waitress and waved his forefinger around in a vague circle.

'We'll start with a couple of bottles of Bolly. What do you say?'

Edward and Eric were still standing, and as the rest of the group settled, Edward stuck his hand across the table to Barbara. 'Hello, nice to see you again. Evening Larry.' Eric followed suit and with the formalities completed, the table fell into polite conversation.

Karen cleared her throat. 'How're you enjoying London, Barbara?'

'*Barb*, please. And London? What's not to love? It's definitely all it's hyped up to be - the epicentre of cool. You gals have it all on your doorstep. The shopping...!' She broke into a grin. 'And Larry tells me y'all are related?'

'Yes,' said Vera, twisting away from the men to join the conversation, 'Edward and Eric are twins, so we're sisters-in-law.'

'And best friends,' added Karen.

'Well I envy you,' said Barbara frankly. 'Swinging London, gorgeous husbands...and look at the pair of you. Beautiful.'

Glasses of champagne appeared.

'Cheers all,' boomed William and everyone stopped to raise their drinks. 'Here's to friendship and prosperity with our friends from across the pond.'

'You know,' said Karen when the clinking of glasses subsided, 'we'd love to spend a day with you before you head home, Barb. We could have lunch, see a show...?'

'Yes,' said Vera, 'sounds great but if it's a weekday, I'd have to be home for the school pick-up.'

Barbara smiled. 'You have kids?'

'Yes, twin boys. They'll be turning six in a couple of weeks.'

'Well of course we can work around their schedule. What about you Karen? Do you have children?'

Karen kept her tone upbeat. 'No, it's just me and Eric.'

'Oh.' Barb took a sip of champagne.

Karen couldn't look at her. She sensed Vera struggling to come up with something to cover the moment. All the men were bantering loudly and Eric actually had his back to the women, now.

'What about you?' said Vera a little belatedly.

'We have Larry Jnr,' said Barbara, proudly. 'My mom is taking care of him while we're on this trip.'

'You must miss him?'

'I really do; he's a honey. Nearly three and full of mischief.'

How could you? thought Karen, *how could you fly halfway round the world and leave your little boy at home?*

'I've got a picture of him in my purse.'

Do not get the photos out. Please don't.

Barb produced a small square snap of a fair-haired, freckle-nosed child in a striped t-shirt and shorts, squinting in bright sunlight. 'This was taken at his very first game...'

Vera jumped in. 'Football?'

'Baseball,' replied Barb with a doting smile. 'Larry got him a catcher's mitt for his birthday; it's the cutest thing. Not that he can catch anything with it, he's just learning his ball skills - Larry's buddy Marv is a Little League coach and he said Junior's got a great eye. He's very young of course, but Larry sure wants him to learn so he's ready to step up to the plate when he's old enough.'

Karen nodded politely hoped Vera would say something to change the subject. Her own mind was a blank.

'How about Monday?' said Vera, 'for our girls day out?'

'Fab!' Barbara lit up. 'Will you come into the city? Show me the sights?'

Karen pulled herself together. 'Yes, let's! We'll come to your hotel if you like and go from there. She glanced at their menfolk, all totally immersed in one another's company, downing drinks and bellowing with laughter. 'We'll leave this lot to their boring business meetings while we go and have fun.' She flashed a bright smile.

Vera caught her eye and gave the smallest nod. *Well done.*

THE TAXI DROPPED Karen and Eric off first. On the pavement, Eric fumbled for his wallet but Edward waved him away.

'I'll get it.'

'Ah cheers, Ed.' He took a small step backwards and tripped on the kerb.

Edward howled with laughter from inside the cab. 'Get him upstairs to bed quick, Karen - he's blitzed!'

Eric sat on the pavement, sniggering weakly.

'G'night Vera,' said Karen. 'Night, Ed.' She walked up the path, unlocked the front door and let herself into the house, made for the stairs and didn't look back.

The cab pulled away and Eric hauled himself to his feet and followed his wife up to their bedroom.

He paused in the doorway, tugging at the knot of his tie.

'What's the matter with you?' He tottered into the room and fell on the bed.

Karen stared at him through her dressing-table mirror where she sat, still in her metallic dress.

'Nothing.' She began applying face cream to remove her make-up.

Eric rolled onto his back. 'You've got a face like a slapped arse. Have had all night.'

Karen finished up at the dressing table and undressed.

'Give us a hand will you?' said Eric blearily, still spread-eagled on the eiderdown.

Karen bent down to pull off his boots and socks.

'Why the silent treatment?' he muttered.

'Did you get the account?' retorted Karen, 'I hope so, you spent enough on liquor, showing off to old Larry Senior.'

'It's in the bag, baybee. What are you so bummed about?'

'I told you. Nothing.'

Karen shoved him onto his side of the bed, climbed in and clicked off the bedside light, somehow unable to tell him that once again, Aunt Flo had come to visit.

THE FOLLOWING MORNING, Eric made a sheepish appearance in the kitchen where Karen was frying bacon and eggs.

He sidled up behind her and nuzzled her neck. 'Morning beautiful.'

She plated up and ducked from under his arms. 'Here, eat this.'

Eric took his seat. 'Sorry about last night,' he said, humbly.

Karen grunted and sat opposite him. She poured tea from the teapot and added two sugars. 'Face like a slapped arse?'

A dark red flush blotted out the greenish tinge to his skin. 'Sorry love.'

Karen folded her arms. 'Was that the booze talking? You should know better than to get plastered, especially in front of a so-called important client.'

Eric pushed down a mouthful of greasy food. 'We had to keep up with Larry, and man can he drink. It'd look bad if we sat there sipping orange juice. What's his missus like?'

'She's nice. American.' *A mother.* 'Me 'n Vera are taking her out for the day on Monday.'

'Aww Kar, you're the best...' Eric put down his cutlery and held out his arms. 'Come here.'

The corners of her mouth softened into a smile. 'Don't push it.'

THREE

Barbara's pillbox hat felt a season or two out of date to Karen. She wondered what their American visitor made of her pastel shift dress and go-go boots, while Vera, stylish as always in a tight sleeveless sweater and frosted lipstick led the charge, expertly hailing a cab outside Barbara's hotel and issuing instructions to the driver.

Barb wanted to go to Hamleys. Of course she did; the biggest toy shop in the world, slap bang in the middle of the West End. The seven levels of fun for Junior sent her into a shopping frenzy.

Karen straightened her spine and got on with it. She picked up a couple of Matchbox cars for Paul and Mark and tried to engage in Barbara and Vera's discussion about G.I. Joe and the next big thing, Action Man. By lunchtime, her face was hurting with the effort of keeping a sunny smile pinned there.

'Pizza Express?' she said when they finally emerged back onto Regent Street.

Barb clapped her hands. 'Hell yeah.'

'To Soho!' cried Vera and threw out her arm for a taxi.

They weaved through London, with Vera and Karen pointing out famous landmarks. 'The Scenic Drive,' Vera called it and they all giggled when the driver seemed to be going out of his way to avoid the most direct route. It would only have taken fifteen minutes to walk there.

KAREN CAUGHT BARB WATCHING HER, over lunch. The pillbox hat was off, the blonde flip-style hair a little tousled and Barbara looked young and happy.

'Tell me a bit about all y'all,' she said, biting into a cheesy slice of pizza. 'You first, Karen.'

Karen leaned back in her seat. 'What you see is what you get, pretty much.'

'What I see is a lovely young women with the world at her feet...'

'Well there you go.'

'...with the prettiest face and cutest smile...'

'Ah, now you're just being nice.'

'...and the deepest, saddest eyes I've ever seen in my life.'

Oblivious to Karen's sinking heart, the noisy pizzeria rose and fell around their table like a fairground carousel. Nobody spoke.

'Well,' said Barbara eventually, 'you can tell me to mind

my nosy American business if you like, but honey I hate to see what I'm seeing in you.'

Mortified her jolly demeanour was so unconvincing, Karen raised her head and met Barbara's bright blue eyes.

'I hope you're not worried about the boys' work,' added Barb. 'Larry is so impressed with them and the agency.' Her voice dropped a notch. 'He hasn't told me outright, but I reckon it's a done deal.'

'It's nothing to do with the account,' mumbled Karen. She glanced at Vera.

'It's....' said Vera and stopped.

'It's personal,' said Karen flatly.

'Sure. Of course, honey.' Barbara drew back.

Trapped between the two women, Karen could hardly just walk out the door. It was so important to create a good impression - she and Vera usually sparkled and Karen could feel her sister-in-law willing her to snap out of her funk. Their job was to give the wives a fun time in London, not subject them to this.

Vera delicately cleared her throat. 'Ladies, I'm so sorry but I have to get the train...the boys...' She tailed off.

Barbara nodded. 'Of course. But we'll catch up again before Larry and I fly home I hope?'

Vera unhooked her bag from the back of the chair and stood. 'Definitely.' She paused. 'Are you coming, Karen?'

What for? To go home in the middle of the afternoon to an empty house?

'Say,' said Barb, 'how about you and I do a little more shopping? I'd love to see some of the famous London boutiques I've heard so much about.' She looked across at Karen with a friendly smile.

Vera shifted from one foot to the other and threw a quick look at the door. 'Karen love? You coming or staying?'

'I'll stay.'

'Fantastic!' said Barb, 'let's go shop up a storm.'

LONDON's soft summer dusk was gathering when the two women emerged from Biba; carrier bags dangling from their hands.

'I could murder a drink,' said Barb, with feeling.

Karen grinned. 'Me too.'

They stopped outside a shoe shop.

'I know of a few bars,' said Karen, eying up a pair of Chelsea Boots for Eric in the window.

Barb hesitated. 'I don't know. Larry mightn't like...'

Karen zoned back in, 'or what about your hotel? The boys will be finishing up for the day soon anyway - they could join us there.'

'Yes,' said Barbara quickly, 'sounds good.'

A friendly voice interrupted them.

'Hello Karen!' A striking man in black motorcycle leathers dashed by, with a wave.

'Hi Roland.'

The man disappeared, leaving Barb open-mouthed.

'Lordy, who was *that*?'

'Roland Phillips-Watson. He's a lovely guy; owns an art gallery in Hampstead.'

'You know him?'

'Well not terribly well. He's a wonderful photographer - quite famous actually.'

'Stop it! Does he take pictures of you?'

'Oh no, we only know one another socially. You know how it is.'

They took a couple of steps.

'So,' said Barb, her bright eyes dancing, 'you're into photography? Or into Roland Phillips-Watson?'

Karen playfully shunted into her. 'I'm married! And it's the art that blows my mind, not the man behind the camera. Although,' she added with a mischievous twinkle, 'I've got to admit, he's easy on the eye.'

Barb let out a guffaw. 'Gotcha.'

'Ha - no really, the London art scene is fantastic,' said Karen. 'There's so much talent out there and I love the idea of minimalism.'

'You do?'

Karen flicked her short straight hair.

'Oh right, yeah. So I guess you and Vera are pretty different in that way.'

'We're different in just about every way you can think of and I adore her. She keeps me sane.'

'She'd probably say the same about you.'

Karen's eyes misted and she blinked quickly. 'Jeez, I'm so emotional all the time,' she muttered. 'Let's get out of here and have something to drink.'

'THE THING IS,' said Barb as they sat in the back of a cab en route to the hotel, 'Larry wouldn't like it if I went to a bar without him - he gets kind of protective. I'm his second wife, actually.'

Karen nodded. She'd suspected a sizeable age gap between the pair and wondered about it.

'He has older kids,' added Barbara. 'Older than Junior I mean. Three of 'em.'

Karen kept a neutral tone. 'Okay. Cool.'

'Yeah, we don't get on. Me and Lenore. She's the first Mrs. Hasting.'

'Ah.'

Barb shot her a sidelong glance. 'She's nasty. A nasty old bitch.'

Karen gasped and bit back a mad titter. She met Barbara's wide-open eyes and saw unconcealed merriment dancing there too.

'It's true,' added Barb, 'but whatever you do, don't tell Larry I said so.'

Karen felt a sudden rush of affection for this bright young woman. Perhaps life with old Larry Hasting wasn't the glamorous round of shopping and parties it seemed. Karen thought about her own marriage. Babies aside, she and Eric had so few problems. They'd grown up in the five years they'd been together and while his career had skyrocketed, he'd never forced her to stay home and be a housewife. It was kind of expected, yes, but she'd wanted that; wanted to be a homemaker for him and their family. She couldn't imagine him clipping her wings, minding about her going for a drink, having a mean ex-wife who'd already successfully raised three kids, bringing her on trips without her son.

Back at the hotel, they settled in at the bar.

'Put it on the room tab,' whispered Barbara.

'I'll have a Bloody Mary please,' said Karen to the bartender. 'And....'

'An Old Fashioned.'

'Coming right up.' The bartender got busy with the drinks.

'We'll be over here.' Karen slithered off the barstool and gestured to a table. She was dying to hear more about the hideous ex-wife. 'Talk to me about life in the States,' she said to Barb, deliberately leaving the conversation wide open.

'Not until you tell me what's bugging you.'

Karen faltered. 'Hmm. Must we go there?'

'Yes,' said Barbara firmly.

'Barb...'

'It might help - a problem shared...'

'Nah. Not in this case.'

'Tell me!'

Karen crumpled. 'We can't have babies,' she muttered eventually. '*I* can't. And yeah I know there are millions of people all round the world in the same boat. I'm not unique, I get it but it's...I'm....'

'Oh honey, I'm sorry.' Barbara paused. 'Jeez, and we just spent all morning in a toy shop.'

'It's okay.'

'No, it isn't.' Barb shifted to the edge of her seat and touched Karen's forearm. 'And you have your two nephews too. That's gotta be so hard.'

Karen gave a sharp shake of her head. 'I love the boys I really do, but Barb my heart is broken. The sadness is like a giant hand squeezing the very life out of me and I don't know what to do.'

'Have you...and I'm sure you have, but honey have you been checked out? Maybe it's Eric?'

'No, it's me. It's my fault.' Karen bit down hard on her lip.

'Don't say that.'

'I'm not a real woman. Women have been getting pregnant since the dawn of time. Women who don't even want babies.' She closed her eyes, a red flush spreading up her neck.

'But Karen, you're so young. Give yourself time.'

Karen gave a miserable shake of her head. 'I'm not as young as I look.' Her voice was getting tight, her face was getting blotchy; she knew it.

Without a word, Barb left the table, went to the bar and came back with two glasses of chilled white wine.

'Or would you prefer something stronger? A Cognac? I could...'

'No, no this is perfect.' The glass touched Karen's lips and as she breathed in the wine's bouquet, tension trickled out of her tight shoulders.

'You know very much about wine?' asked Barb.

'God no, I'll drink anything.'

'When you come to the States, which I hope you will one

day, we'll go on a trip to California. Then you'll see the difference.'

Karen studied her. 'D'you think the boys will work together in the future?'

'For sure. Larry is so energised by Ed and Eric's enthusiasm, their passion...I gotta tell you, this whole town feels optimistic.' She fished about in her bag. 'Cigarette?' A pack of Hasting's appeared and a dainty silver lighter.

'That's pretty.' Karen put a cigarette between her lips and Barbara lit it for her. She took a deep drag and as she exhaled, felt the knots in her neck muscles loosening.

'Sorry about earlier,' she said softly with a quick glance around the bar.

'Nothing to apologise for. I know what it's like to have problems you can't control.'

'Mmm.'

Barb expertly flicked ash into a large ceramic ashtray bearing the hotel's tan and cream logo. 'Have you thought about adopting?'

Karen nodded. 'Of course.'

'But?'

'Look, it's not an easy path - and who knows, maybe one day we'll try - but honestly, we want out own baby.'

'Yeah.'

A clatter of voices broke into their thoughts.

'Good evening, ladies!' Eric strode across the bar, closely followed by Edward and Larry. All three were carrying beers. Eric leaned down and planted a warm kiss on Karen's cheek. 'Hello darling.' He straightened. 'Evening Barbara.'

Barb gave a ladylike nod of her head. 'Hi guys.'

'Wow,' said Ed, catching sight of the shopping bags under the table. 'You've been busy.'

'Uh huh. We had fun. I adore London.'

Larry gave an exaggerated groan. 'See what happens when I'm hard at work? I'll be penniless if we stay here much longer. Karen m'dear you're a bad influence.' He winked.

'Vera went home after lunch,' said Karen to Ed as he dragged extra chairs from the adjoining table and the men squashed themselves in.

'Right.'

Larry twisted round in his seat. 'This place got a decent restaurant? We should grab some dinner. Everyone hungry?'

FOUR

'You like her, don't you?' said Eric as he and Karen got ready for bed.

'Barb? Yeah, she's cool.'

'When we got to the bar, you two were deep in conversation. Like best mates.'

Karen pulled back the covers and slipped into bed. 'She's easy to talk to.'

'These are new.' Eric reached out and touched the frill on Karen's pink babydoll pyjamas.

'Yep. Got them today.'

'Cute.'

The word sat awkwardly for Karen. 'I think I'm too old to be cute.'

Eric propped himself up on one elbow, a furrow appearing between his eyes. 'You're not old. Not even close to being old. What's brought this on?'

Karen shrugged. 'I feel like life's passing me by.'

'Are you serious?'

'It doesn't matter.'

'Yes it does. Come here.' He pulled her close and she felt the heat from his body through the chiffon fabric of her top. She felt childish and needy. Weak, even.

'You can do anything you like, Karen. What is it you want? We're doing alright for money.'

She wriggled away from him. 'You know what I want.'

He gave a deep, sorrowful sigh. 'I can't fix that though, can I love?'

'I might go to California,' she said abruptly.

'What?'

'Nothing.'

'Has Barbara said something to upset you?'

Karen gave a short laugh. 'It's got nothing to do with Barbara.'

Eric flopped onto his back and stared up into the darkness.

'Larry's an arrogant arsehole,' he said.

'I thought you liked him.'

'That's before I got to know him. He has plenty of cash and likes what we're doing with the campaign so...'

'Well I actually do like Barbara.'

'Okay. Well good for you.'

Silence fell.

'They'll be gone in a couple of weeks anyway,' said Eric.

Karen thought about Barb going home and seeing her son. She pictured the scene...the freckly little boy in the stripy t-shirt running out of a huge white mansion with Barb's mother, a stylish woman in her sixties perhaps, leaning on the doorframe in twinset and pearls, laughing happily as Barb and Junior embrace on the lawn. Barb would pick him up and cover his face with pink-lipsticked kisses.

'Where in the States do they live?' she asked Eric now.

'Manhattan.'

Karen gave a small rueful smile, her mental picture dissolving from colonial grandeur to trendy city apartment. Different setting, but same people, same feelings. Something she would never know.

She lay flat on her back next to her husband, knowing sleep was nowhere. Eric moved closer and found her hand.

'Don't torture yourself darling,' he whispered. 'We can still be happy, can't we? I love you so much.'

Tears burned behind Karen's wide-open eyes. Eric knew her sadness, he knew her pain and the knowledge didn't come alone; he also knew he couldn't take the sorrow away. He shared in Karen's desolation, so how could she lie here and tell this beautiful man that for her, he could never ever be enough?

'I love you too,' she said as she had time and again, month after month, year after year. It never stopped hurting, it only seemed to get worse; this thing that was bigger than both of them. They could never overcome it, the only option was to accept it and make the best of what they had. The swollen tears slid slowly over her temples and into her hair, but she made no sound at all.

THROUGH THEIR HUSBANDS' office, plans were made for Vera, Karen and Barb to meet up again, this time for a trip to the theatre and dinner. Dorothy the secretary booked the tickets.

There was a musical playing at the Prince of Wales Theatre. *Passion Flower Hotel* sounded a little risqué and fun and Karen found herself looking forward to an evening out with the girls. Larry Hasting might be coming round to the idea of Barb having a life of her own, she thought, or perhaps he'd decided Vera and Karen were trustworthy. Either way, it was liberating to think there'd be no meet up later with the men; Ed had secured VIP tickets for them at the boxing.

Saturday night rolled around and Karen and Vera walked up to the station for the Waterloo train.

'You okay?' asked Vera as they settled into their seats. The guard blew the whistle and the train pulled away from the platform, gradually gathering speed.

Karen gazed through the grimy window and saw her own pale reflection staring back at her, as the lengthening shadows outside drew the evening closer.

'I'm alright. Tonight will be fun.'

Vera pressed again. 'Have you and Eric had a fight?'

Karen pulled her eyes away from the glass. 'No.'

'What then? You don't want to go out?'

'Why are you asking?'

Vera hesitated. 'You seem distant. Distracted.'

Karen inhaled and let the breath out slowly, as though

playing for time. 'There's nothing new. Just the usual; my period came the other day.'

'Ah.' Vera gave a kind, closed-lip smile. 'I really wish there was something I could do. I mean it, Karen. Me and Ed, we feel so sad about it all.'

'I know. Thank you.'

'It's so unfair.'

'Mmm.'

Silence fell between them, as the train rattled its way through the outer London suburbs towards the dazzling lights of the city.

PASSION FLOWER HOTEL was light and easy but fell short of the sexed-up romp the posters had suggested. Karen was glad; on reflection, the idea of teenage girls basically prostituting themselves to their male boarding school counterparts in order to lose their virginity really did seem quite tasteless. She flicked through the programme during the interval, admiring the simple motifs and fresh young palette. The font was cool, too.

Vera and Barb had ostensibly gone to the ladies' but Karen wasn't in the least bit surprised when they arrived back inside the auditorium a few minutes after the second half had started, giggling and apologising as fellow patrons were obliged to stand up to allow them access to their row.

Vera dropped into her seat and Karen caught hints of

cigarette smoke and alcohol. She felt like a party pooper and resolved to suggest going for cocktails before dinner.

THEY WERE two drinks in before Barbara brought up the subject Karen dreaded, but a couple of cocktails on an empty stomach had left her feeling slightly light-headed. Her guard was down.

'Karen,' began Barb a little hesitantly, 'I think you guys are fantastic. You and Eric are like the perfect couple.'

'Hey!' Vera snorted into her drink.

'As are you and Ed of course.' Barb coloured up, unsure how to take Vera's forthright manner. 'But we're discussing this pair right now, aren't we?' She inched closer to the two other women.

Karen rolled her eyes. 'We don't have to talk about this, surely?' She tipped her glass. 'Let's have a few more of these and go for dinner. I'm starving.'

'I'm sorry Karen, but I want to help. You gals have been so kind to me, you have no idea how good it is to be out from Larry's scrutiny. Or worse, Lenore's.'

'You've got your own friends, though? Back at home I mean,' said Vera.

Barb's crimson blush deepened. 'Not really. Well yes of course I have acquaintances, but not what you'd call pals.'

'Well get out there girl and do something about it.'

'Vera honey, I would but it's...difficult.'

'Larry?' prompted Karen.

'Look, I don't want to sound disloyal, or ungrateful...'

'Ungrateful?' Vera's eyes widened. She glanced at Karen.

Clearly uncomfortable now, Barbara fidgeted with the straw in her drink for a moment, long fair hair falling over part of her face.

'It's complicated.'

'What is?' demanded Vera.

Karen gave a soft cough. 'Do you feel like you're a little bit under the thumb, Barb? Seeing as how Larry's so much older than you.'

The blond head nodded sadly.

'He's a control freak?' Vera sounded genuinely shocked. 'He seems like such a nice man.'

'Don't be fooled by appearances. *Controlling* is putting it mildly.' Barb's baby blue eyes were full. 'Ah Jeez, I mustn't drink any more.'

A slightly awkward pause arose.

'Can we not talk about it?' whispered Barbara eventually.

'Well,' said Vera, 'if we can't talk about Karen's problems and we can't talk about your problems, then what *can* we talk about?'

Karen broke into a grin. 'I reckon it's time to talk about *your* problems.'

'Ha! Okay well how about this for starters? Ed's never home before 7.00pm.'

'Same,' interrupted Karen. 'What else?'

'And when he is home, all he wants to do is sleep. And I mean *sleep*.'

'Same. You'll have to do better than that.'

'And he flips his wig every now and again when he looks at the cheque book stubs...'

'Same,' said Barb under her breath.

Karen downed her cocktail. 'Yeah, I can just see Ed getting the hump with you over money. Over *anything* in fact. Flips his wig actually means he says you look gorgeous every minute of the day, he loves you more than life itself and wants to give you the world.'

The sisters-in-law chuckled over the ridiculousness of Vera's so-called problems.

'Not same.'

The laughter stopped abruptly when they realised what Barbara had said.

'Oh Barb,' said Karen. She reached out and took her hand. Vera covered them with both of hers and the three women sat linked together amid their empty cocktail glasses as the tender shoots of friendship were forged into bonds.

FIVE

One last catch-up was arranged before Larry and Barb flew back to America. With the advertising account safely signed and sealed, Eric and Ed were jubilant.

A farewell dinner, hosted by the big boss William Shepherd and his wife Doreen at their home in Richmond was scheduled for the night before the Americans left London. Vera and Karen were keen to spend time with Barbara; just the three of them.

'Let's go ice-skating,' said Vera over cups of tea in Karen's kitchen two days prior to the dinner. 'Us girls could go to the rink in the afternoon and then to William's for dinner afterwards; it's not far from there.'

'Yeah I'd love to. Skating's a gas.'

'I'll ring the office,' said Vera 'and ask Dorothy to get a message to Barb.'

'Doting Dot,' said Karen, not unkindly. 'She bloody loves our boys; do anything for them.'

'Yeah, she's fab. Sorting out their wives' social life is probably not part of her job description.'

Karen made the peace sign, 'she's outta sight.'

'Man, I hope she never leaves. The office would fall apart without her,' said Vera.

'So you'll ring and arrange it?'

'Yep, and I'll organise Anna to babysit Mark and Paul. I hope she'll be free...I've booked her twice this week already.'

Karen moved swiftly on. 'Ice skating,' she said, 'I'm jazzed.'

THE AFTERNOON at the rink was brilliant fun and Barb turned out to be a pretty good skater.

'New York winters, y'all,' she said by way of explanation.

The sisters-in-law discovered both Barbara and Larry were in fact from the south originally, but work had taken them all over the country and nowadays they were prominent figures on the New York social scene. Karen had the sense that Larry had been angling to get to the Big Apple for some time because his three older children and ex-wife lived just a few hours out of the city. She wondered if living in the buzzing metropolis made Barb feel like a fish out of water. A Southern Belle in Manhattan. Karen, so often at odds with her own life, identified with this.

The three women spent a couple of hours at the rink in

Richmond and at 5.00pm, skated to the barrier, pink-cheeked and exhilarated and clumped their way to the lockers to retrieve their shoes and bags.

Vera sank onto a wooden bench to remove her skates, tugging at the knots in her laces.

'Let's go somewhere,' she puffed, 'before showing up at William's.'

Karen freed herself from her skates and slipped gratefully into a pair of cool green sling-backs.

'Yes, let's go for a drink,' she said, checking her watch. 'We've got plenty of time. There's a nice pub on the hill.' She glanced at Barb, whose face was hidden behind her hair as she bent to remove her own skates. 'It's not rough or anything,' she added.

'Not in this area,' said Vera. 'Millionaire's Row.'

Barb straightened. 'No sweat, I know you'd never take me to some dive. I wanna get dressed properly for dinner, though.' She faced the others. 'And let's keep this between us girls, okay? No need for Larry to know we stopped off at a bar.'

'He won't hear it from us,' said Vera and waved a hand at their bags. 'We'll get all our gear sorted at the pub and the old man will be none the wiser.' She patted her up-do, which looked slightly the worse for wear. 'Thank God I brought hairspray.'

'WHAT TIME'S YOUR FLIGHT TOMORROW?' asked Karen as she and Barbara settled into the snug at The Wintermoon.

'The morning. Early.' Barb took a sip of her Pimms.

'Aww, we'll miss you. It's been fab having you here,' said Karen and then remembered to add, 'but you'll get to see Junior.'

Barb put her drink down. 'There's something I want to say. I've been wanting to say it for a while, but it's kinda now or never.'

Karen glanced over her shoulder. 'Let's wait for Vera - she won't be much longer.' If the thing on Barb's mind had anything to do with Junior, then Karen wanted backup. She didn't feel equipped to offer advice or even an opinion on anything to do with parenting.

'Honey, it's you I want to talk about.'

Karen took a hefty slug from her glass. 'Oh man, we've spent far too much time talking about me already,' she said lightly. 'I don't want your last night here to be bogged down in...'

'Listen,' interrupted Barbara. 'It's not something I think Vera should hear until you've had a chance to think about it.'

Uneasiness stirred in Karen's gut. 'Barb...'

'Hear me out,' said Barbara urgently, 'please.'

Something in her tone scattered pinpricks over Karen's scalp. 'No,' she said firmly, 'whatever it is, I want Vera here.'

'And here I am!' Vera appeared at the table on a waft of perfume, immaculately dressed in a black lace dress and sparkly tights. 'Sorry I took so long.' She slithered onto the curved velvet-covered seat next to Karen. 'What's happening?'

Karen leaned back. She didn't know what to say and covered the moment by taking a cigarette from the open pack on the table.

Vera eyed the two women. 'Well?'

Barbara shifted in her seat.

'One of you say something,' said Vera. 'You couldn't look more uptight if you tried. What's going on?'

Karen exhaled and a bloom of cigarette smoke floated over the table. 'Barb?' she said pointedly.

'You don't like the dress?' said Vera. 'C'mon, you can tell me. My hair?' She touched the masterpiece of backcombing on her head. 'What? You're freaking me out.'

'You look beautiful, Vera,' murmured Barbara. 'I just...God, I don't know how to...'

Karen sat back, smoking. A feeling of apprehension fluttered up inside and it seemed important to keep a neutral expression. She took another drag, feigning nonchalance.

Vera's expression hardened. 'This is bullshit,' she muttered. 'If you want me to leave, just say so.'

'No,' said Barbara quickly, 'I'm sorry. Jeez I wish I hadn't...'

'Spit it out.' Karen extinguished her half-smoked cigarette. 'Please.'

Barbara's huge, kohl-rimmed eyes were filled with trepidation. 'Okay.' She cleared her throat. 'Well here's the thing.'

The others waited.

'It's about having babies.'

'I knew it!' Karen snatched up her drink. 'For the love of God...'

'Karen, *please* don't get upset. I only want to help.'

Vera inhaled sharply. 'Barbara, it's *not* helpful to keep going on about it. Can't you see how much it hurts Karen?'

'Yeah, but that's just the point. I think I know of a way...' she lowered her voice, 'for you to be a mother.'

Karen's head jerked up. 'If you've got some crazy black-market American drug you think I should take, then I'm telling you now, I'm not gonna do it. I've heard about these things.'

'It's not drugs,' said Vera, 'I can tell by her face. It's even worse.'

'Jesus Christ! What do you mean?'

'I think she means illegal adopting,' said Vera darkly. '*Buying* a baby.'

Karen gasped.

'No...listen,' hissed Barbara. 'Listen to me. I'm talking about somebody having a baby *for* you.'

There was a beat.

'What the fuck?' mumbled Vera.

Barbara inched closer. 'I've given it a lot of thought, and Karen sweetheart you told me yourself it's you who can't have babies. Not Eric.'

'Yeah? So?'

'Well, think about it. If Eric could have a baby without you, then technically it would still be your child, right?'

'Without me? No no no....' Karen sat up. 'No you don't.

That means Eric would have to sleep with some other woman and I'm telling you now, that is not happening.'

Vera shook her head. 'I've gotta say, Barb, I'm kind of shocked. Why the hell would you even suggest such a thing?'

Barbara had her answer ready. 'But what if the other woman was someone Karen trusts and respects?'

'Someone you trust and respect is unlikely to go off and shag your husband,' said Karen hotly.

'I need you to think outside the box,' insisted Barb. Her persistence was sowing uncomfortable seeds. Karen gave a quick shake of her head.

'Let's move on, girls.'

'But Karen,' Barb's tone was low and insistent, 'what if the woman is someone you *love*?'

'What?'

It took a moment for the penny to drop.

'Oh my God, Vera,' said Karen, turning saucer-eyed to her sister-in-law. 'She means you.'

SIX

There was a stunned silence. And then Barbara scrambled to her feet and fled the Snug, leaving Vera and Karen staring at one another, aghast.

'Bloody hell.' Vera lit a cigarette.

Karen took it from her.

'Bloody hell,' said Vera again. 'I mean...'

Karen inhaled and passed the cigarette back. 'How dare she?' It was barely above a whisper.

Vera shook her head.

The air was thick with cigarette smoke and tension. Karen started to feel claustrophobic.

'Are you okay?' said Vera.

'Are you?'

'I don't know.'

'Me neither.'

'Wow, I mean - it's a ridiculous idea.'

'Who does she think she is? I mean seriously, *as if...*'

Vera raised her shoulders.

'Don't take that the wrong way,' added Karen hastily, 'I reckon *any* bloke would want to, you know, sleep with you.'

'Yeah but your Eric and me...?' Vera tailed off; the thought left dangling so alien and bizarre.

'And to what end?' said Karen slowly. 'To make a baby? Make a baby for *me*?' She shuddered. 'That's insane.'

They sat for a few moments in silence as the dust of Barbara's explosive proposition settled.

Vera shifted. 'Where did she go?'

'Back to America I hope,' said Karen, harshly. 'I doubt she'll show her face here again.'

'She'll have to,' said Vera, 'we've got the dinner tonight, at William's.' She paused. 'I'd better go and look for her.'

'Leave it.'

Vera stood up. 'Just forget she ever said anything. We'll get through tonight, play nice with Barb and Larry, and then we don't have to think about these people ever again. The boys have got the account so that's the main thing.' She left the Snug, disappearing into the noisy main bar.

Karen picked up her drink. Alcohol mixed with the recently smoked cigarette left a bitter taste in her mouth. She felt jolted and uneasy; the thought of Eric and Vera together made her sick. Vera had said to forget about it, but how could she? The facts were irrefutable - Karen was the one who couldn't have a baby, not Eric. A sly, terrifying thought wormed its way into Karen's brain; maybe one day Eric's desire to be a father would become so powerful, it might cause him to leave her and find a woman who could bear children. He said all the right things, never showed a sliver of interest in being jealous of his brother, showered Karen with love and affection, but *what if* all that changed one day? Goosebumps stood out on her forearms.

She looked up at a movement in the doorway and saw Vera entering the Snug with Barbara in her wake. Karen couldn't read Vera's expression, but Barbara looked devastated. They slid back onto the seat in silence.

Barb lifted heavy eyes. 'I'm sorry Karen,' she said hoarsely. 'I really only want to help. It came out all wrong.'

Karen folded her lips together. Her heart was bumping.

Vera picked up her Pimms. 'We won't mention it again, okay? Karen...Barbara...we've gotta get through this evening and then tomorrow you guys will fly back to New York and we'll all just get on with our lives.'

Silence.

'Okay?'

'Of course,' muttered Barb.

Karen forced herself to look at her. 'This thing you're talking about,' she said. 'Is it common in the States?'

Vera gulped. 'Karen love...don't...'

'Is it?' Karen fixed Barbara with a hard stare.

Barbara glanced anxiously from one woman to the other. 'Well it can actually be traced back to biblical times,' she said carefully. 'Usually with...with family members.'

'Enough!' snapped Vera. 'We're not living in *biblical* times.'

Despite herself, Karen leaned closer. 'Is it legal?'

Barb gazed at her, confused. 'Uh, no I don't think so.' She paused. 'But I've heard of people doing it anyway.'

'Time to go,' said Vera briskly. She stood and shouldered her bag. 'Come on ladies, or we'll be late for dinner.'

THE PRAWN COCKTAIL STARTER, followed by Coq au Vin prepared by Doreen Shepherd looked delicious, but to Karen, everything tasted of cardboard. Her mouth was paper-dry, whereas Vera carried on seemingly as normal - gregarious and charming. She had the whole table in fits over some hilarious anecdote Karen was sure she was making up on the spot. And Barbara sat quietly, eating little and barely able to make eye contact with the others.

'Worried about the flight tomorrow, dear?' Doreen eyed Barb's full plate, as she removed the dishes. She patted her hand. 'Never mind. There's Black Forest Gateau for dessert.'

'Thank you Mrs. Shepherd, I guess I'm just not very hungry,' said Barbara, dabbing at her lips with a white linen napkin.

'Well,' said Doreen kindly, 'it's been a very busy few weeks for you I'm sure. I expect you'll be happy to go home to your little boy?'

Barb risked a fleeting glance at Karen. 'Of course,' she murmured.

'And the Rabbi said 'you call THAT a matzah ball?'' Vera's latest story reached its climax and the men howled with laughter. She downed a third glass of Blue Nun and joined in, a rosy sheen dusting the tops of her cheekbones, her eyes a little too glittery.

Karen observed the raucous goings-on from under her thick black eyelashes; aware of Eric sending quizzical looks her way from across the table. When they'd arrived at the Shepherd residence, she'd noted with a sinking heart that Doreen had put Vera and Eric next to one another at the table. Karen found herself lumbered with Larry Hasting on one side and William Shepherd on the other. Pleasantries aside, the two men had spoken across Karen virtually all night, but she didn't particularly care. She wasn't in the mood for polite chitchat.

The evening finally dragged to a close and the guests stood in the hallway, shrugging into coats and thanking their hosts. A black cab rumbled at the kerb, ready to whisk Larry and Barb back to their hotel. A second taxi was on the way for Vera, Karen and their husbands. Karen accepted a powdery kiss from Doreen, managed to duck old man Shepherd's wet grey lips, and waited on the driveway.

As Barbara walked past on her way to the cab, she stopped and hugged Karen hard.

'It was lovely to meet you,' she whispered close to Karen's ear. 'I hope we can still be friends.'

'It was nice to meet you, too,' replied Karen formally and then 'of course we're friends. None of this is your fault; I know you're only trying to help. Thank you for caring, Barb. I mean it.'

Relief flooded Barbara's pale face. 'Thank you honey.'

Vera joined them. 'Where's my hug?'

'Oh Vera, you gorgeous creature,' murmured Barbara, 'you're such a doll.'

'Actually,' said Vera cheerfully, 'I'm a bit pissed. But hey ho - we got through the evening, girls.'

The three women embraced and the hard lump in Karen's heart melted away. 'We'll miss you,' she mumbled into Barbara's hair. 'Keep in touch, okay?'

'Barbara!' Larry Hasting was holding the taxi door open. 'Hurry up. Time is money.'

The women laughed politely on cue and Barbara peeled away. 'See you, gals.' She blew them a kiss and climbed into the cab.

SEVEN

K aren undressed slowly. Her overworked brain was
fried. Clashing emotions threatened to swamp her.
She observed her husband, as he got ready for bed, too.

'Thank God that's over,' he muttered as he pulled off his
tie and tossed it in the general direction of the bedroom chair.

Karen automatically padded over the carpet, retrieved the
tie and hung it up.

'You did really well,' she said as she closed the wardrobe
door, 'to get the account.'

'It wasn't just me,' said Eric. 'Ed did a mountain of work
and you girls treated Larry's wife royally. I think they were
very impressed.'

'We weren't trying to impress her,' said Karen, 'she's a
genuinely nice woman. I don't think she has an easy time of it
with Larry, actually.'

'Yeah I'd say life with the old fella is no picnic but hey, she made her bed.' Eric finished undressing. 'Gonna brush my teeth,' he said and went out of the bedroom, leaving Karen standing by the wardrobe in her slip.

The room felt stuffy, even a little oppressive. She opened a window and the velvet night rolled in. Karen inhaled and cricked her neck, trying to dissolve some of the tension stuck there.

When Eric came back she was already in bed. He slid in alongside and reached for her hand.

'Oh.' He stopped.

Karen's heart swelled at his gentlemanly manner; his surprise at finding her hands loosely linked across her naked stomach under the sheet.

'It's okay,' she whispered and heard his breathing change.

'I thought you didn't want...' he started.

Karen bit her lip in the dark. 'What I don't want, is the disappointment month after month,' she said, 'and the horrible reminder that I can't be a mum - so sometimes I feel like it's easier not to try.'

'Oh Kar.' Eric's kind voice made her want to cry.

'It's not that I don't want *you*,' she said, trying to unscramble her thoughts. 'Do you know what I mean?'

He paused. 'In a way.'

His honesty was sweet. He wasn't going to say he understood, just to appease her. Karen thought of other men; Larry Hasting perhaps, maybe even Edward who might have found a string of slick assurances so easy to dish out, in order to move on to them actually having sex.

Karen had always felt safe with Eric. They'd grown up together.

'I love you,' she said, 'and I'm so sorry.'

'Sorry for what?' He gently pulled her closer. 'Sorry for something that isn't meant to be? Sorry for the way you're made? You're perfect. I love you the way you are.'

'You deserve more though. More than I can give you.'

'Don't say that.' Eric cradled her face in his hands and kissed her. 'No tears now, you hear? Please don't cry sweetheart.'

But Karen was beaten. The nightmare scenario created by Barbara mocked her cold despair and sharpened again the pain of her infertility, her sadness for Eric, her love for him and for Vera. And for a baby who would never be born.

EIGHT

Karen's nephews Paul and Mark turned six and their birthday party was scheduled for the Saturday after Barb and Larry flew back to America.

Just before 3.00pm, Karen and Eric walked down the road to Ed and Vera's house. Karen was carrying a tin of mini sausage rolls and a glass bowl of fruit salad, her contribution to the party and Eric struggled with an unwieldy box of Scalextric and two birthday cards.

Ed answered the door, closely followed by a gaggle of excited children.

'Presents!' yelled Paul, darting forwards.

Mark shoved his way to the front of the group. 'Wait for me!'

'Hey, manners.' Ed marched his sons into the sitting room while the rest of the kids bounded back down the hallway. 'Let's start again, shall we?' he said, sternly.

'Hello Auntie Karen,' recited the twins in unison, 'hello Uncle Eric.'

Karen handed the containers of food to Ed and knelt on the carpet. The boys rushed over and she hugged them.

'Hello you two,' she said and kissed them in turn on the cheek. 'Happy birthday!'

'Thank you Auntie Karen,' they chorused, glancing at the big box lying over Eric's knees. 'Thank you Uncle.'

Eric gave them a wink. 'Looks like you're having a great birthday.' Edward retrieved the Scalextric box. 'Thanks guys,' he said and then to his boys, 'we'll save this for later. You can open it after the party.'

The twins opened their mouths to object, but caught their father's eye in time.

'Yes Dad.'

'Yes Dad.'

Ed opened the sitting room door. 'Go and find your friends now. Mum said we'll have tea soon.'

The kids hurtled out, whooping.

Edward sank onto an armchair. 'I'm done in.'

Karen got to her feet, smiling. 'Poor old you.'

He groaned. 'These kids are going apeshit.'

'Where's Vera?'

'Out the back having a sneaky puff, last time I saw her,' said Edward. 'Her nerves are shot, God bless her.'

'Nothing a quick gin and orange won't fix,' said Eric.

'Bloody good idea,' said Edward. 'I'll get us all one.'

Karen made for the door. 'I'm gonna look for Vera.'

'Don't,' muttered Edward, 'you'll get roped into organising

musical bumps or something. One of the little bastards has already spewed up on the carpet.'

Karen grinned. 'It's fine. I'm certain we'll manage.'

In the kitchen, she found Vera looking harassed as she presided over a table of party food.

'Hi!' She lit up at the sight of her sister-in-law and gave her a kiss.

'You okay?' said Karen, 'Ed's getting us a drink.'

'Hallelujah, I'm beat.'

'How's the party going?'

Vera rolled her eyes as deafening pop music, accompanied by ten shrieking six-year-olds thumped out of the record player in the next room.

'One of the little girls threw up. Her mother knows Ossie Clark apparently. Just my luck if Julie was sick on one of his dresses.'

'Ah, I thought it was the carpet.'

'And then one of the boys walloped this other kid with a cricket bat. Well walloped might be a bit strong but anyway, she screamed the house down until we all sat on the floor and played pass-the-parcel and of course I had to make sure she won the tub of Play Doh at the end. And then she took the Play Doh and fucking stuck it on the wallpaper. Little madam. Anyway, Anna's in there with them now.' She jerked her head towards the racket next door. 'Can you tell? She's playing all her favourites. Jesus - she even brought her own records. Move in, why don't you, Anna?'

Karen sat at the kitchen table, picking at a cheese straw and smiling as Vera ranted.

'D'you like the cake?' She pointed at an enormous deco-rated birthday cake in the middle of the table. Paul and Mark's names were picked out in blue icing on the top. Six candles surrounded each name.

'Impressive,' said Karen.

Vera picked up her pack of cigarettes. 'I didn't make it.'

'Oh okay.'

'God, can you imagine me having the patience to do all that piping?'

'You'd be great.'

Vera huffed. 'I don't think so. I feel like a big fat failure today.'

'Don't be silly. You're amazing.'

Vera dropped onto a chair at the table. She looked at the box of cigarettes in her hand. 'I'm getting a bit too attached to these things, but I bloody need them sometimes. Ed reckons I'm addicted.'

'Well, you're not. And it's better than being on Valium isn't it?'

'Ha, mother's little helper.' Vera sighed. 'Anyway,' she said, 'how are you?'

'I'm good.'

Vera lit a cigarette. 'I've been thinking.'

'Uh huh?'

'About what Barbara said.'

Karen's eyes flicked to the open kitchen door. 'Not here,' she murmured.

'No.' Vera pushed back her chair and stood. 'Not here, but I do want to talk to you.'

Spidery fingers ran across Karen's shoulder blades. 'I'm not agreeing to anything,' she said quickly.

'No, of course not. I just think we should talk about what happened. We were both there when Barb said what she said but you and I haven't mentioned it since. We can't have it hanging there.'

'There's nothing to say. It's not happening.'

Vera's eyebrows rose. 'I know.'

The air stilled.

Karen cleared her throat. 'Sorry to snap.'

'It's just...' Vera stopped. 'Well...*could* it work?'

Karen stared at her, bewildered. 'You want to take this seriously?'

'No....'

'But?'

'But I'm starting to think we should talk about it a bit more. Or at least,' she added hastily, 'check it out. What if it's legal? You're the one who asked Barbara about that and even if it's banned in America, it might be permitted somewhere else.'

'Vera,' Karen leaned in, 'what the hell are you talking about?'

'Well...possibilities...'

'I'm not listening to this.' Karen jumped up and lurched into Ed and Eric who were coming into the kitchen with a couple of drinks in their hands.

'Whoa, steady on.' Eric swerved slightly.

Red faced and flustered, Karen pushed past the brothers.

'I'm getting the children in for tea,' she muttered and vanished through the kitchen door.

Out in the hallway, it was cooler. Karen sank onto the bottom stair and her head slid into her hands. The sitting room door was closed, but party games were clearly still in full swing.

'Stop! In the name of love,' commanded The Supremes and each time there was a break in the music, Anna's young voice called out a name. 'Elizabeth! John!' Edward had been right about the musical bumps.

Karen closed her eyes, picturing for the millionth time a child of her own; the birthdays and Christmases and family holidays. Day to day life with a baby in the house. Crooning lullabies, gently rocking, soothing, protecting, loving. Karen's arms ached anew.

Possibilities, Vera said just now. The word sat in Karen's head; tempting, agonisingly close.

She thought about making a baby. When you stripped it back to its barest form, creating life took so little time. A few minutes, if that. And then there'd be a child in the world for a whole lifetime. Could Karen stomach the thought of those scant little seconds if it meant she could be a mother and Eric could be a father? Could she close off her mind and look away, just for a moment? Blink! And it would all be over.

KAREN, Eric and Edward sat in the lounge, amid the debris of Paul and Mark's present-opening extravaganza. Wrapping paper and cards were strewn all over the floor. A thick smear of blue icing clogged the tufts in the carpet and cake crumbs littered the ground like confetti.

At last, tea was over, all the party guests had been collected and the two overtired and now cantankerous birthday boys were in bed. The last twenty minutes had seen both Vera and Ed's patience stretched very thin; there was almost a punch-up over whose Scalextric car was whose and the long day all but ended in tears.

Vera pushed open the sitting room door looking exhausted, and flopped down on the sofa next to Ed.

'Mission accomplished, they are finally asleep,' she announced.

'Here.' Edward put a drink in her hand. She took it, gratefully.

Karen picked up a discarded red Etch A Sketch, smartly packaged in yellow and blue with the promise of "unlimited design possibilities" printed on the side. Possibilities - that word, again.

'Did you make a list of which gift came from which guest?' she said.

Vera gave her a withering look. 'Did you?'

Karen grinned and started to gather rubbish.

'Leave the mess, Kar,' said Edward. 'We'll do it in the morning.'

Vera put her drink down. 'We,' she said and rolled her eyes.

Karen carried on tidying up. She knew Edward had no intention of doing any housework, he never did. But Karen wanted to give Vera a hand; she felt miserable about her attitude earlier. Vera only wanted to offer support and she'd bitten her head off about it.

'Does anyone want anything to eat?' said Vera. 'There are a few sandwiches left, a couple of iced buns.'

There was no response from the others.

'Oh well then, we may as well keep drinking,' she said. 'Fine by me.'

NINE

Daytime drinking agreed with Karen, she decided. A lovely loose-limbed, spacey feeling of freedom was swimming through her entire body. Vera seemed unaffected by numerous glasses of alcohol, with the only hint at inebriation being a pretty pink flush to her cheeks. Ed and Eric got funnier and louder. Karen was glad her husband was a happy drunk.

The measures were sloppy and unchecked. God only knew how much they had all consumed, but Karen didn't care. She felt liberated.

The boys were on a roll. Story after story about clients, deadlines, office gossip. The girls leaned in, rewarding their menfolk with bubbling giggles and shiny-eyed admiration.

Anna peeked around the sitting room door, with her coat on. 'Goodnight, all.'

Vera got clumsily to her feet. 'Thanks for today, sweetie. Let me pay you. Get your wallet out, Ed.'

Anna gave a polite smile. 'It's okay, I'll pick it up tomorrow.'

'Righty-o,' said Edward, slumping back into his seat. 'See ya, doll.'

She raised her hand in a small wave. 'G'night.' The sitting room door clicked shut.

'So,' said Edward as he lit a cigarette, 'what's news with you girls?'

'Yeah,' said Eric, 'I want to hear about the Americans. Dish the dirt, Karen.'

'Well I didn't think much of Larry.'

'Nor me,' said Vera with a shudder. 'If it wasn't for his enormous stash of money, I wouldn't want to know.'

'Now now,' said Edward affectionately, 'money isn't everything.'

'You've changed your tune,' said Eric. 'You told me yourself the only reason you were putting up with the randy old goat was to get the account.'

They all laughed at this. And then.

'Randy?' said Karen.

The twins shared a quick look.

'Let's just say he has an eye for the ladies,' said Eric.

'Gawd, poor Barb.' Vera clicked her cigarette lighter.

'Ah yes, Sweet Cheeks,' said Edward, 'what did you find out about her? She's a bit young for him don't you think?'

'Never mind too young, she's too *good* for him,' said Karen indignantly.

'She does alright.'

Karen didn't like the hardened tone of his voice.

'Barbara's very kind,' she retorted, 'she cares about people.'

'She cares about you,' said Vera, firmly.

'Oh yeah, how so?' Eric got up and wandered over to the cocktail cabinet. 'Who wants what?'

'Top me up will you?' Vera held out her glass.

'Karen?'

'I'm okay.'

'You're not okay though, are you?' said Vera, seemingly oblivious. 'You're only feeling good because of how much we've had to drink today.'

Karen gave a shallow laugh. 'That's a bit rich.'

Vera shrugged. 'It's no secret I'll get legless with the best of them, but you're always so careful. When's the last time you let your hair down and got totally trashed?'

Karen's shoulder twitched. She couldn't answer.

'See, there's no reason for you to be leading this miserable life.'

'Vera!' Karen paled.

'Well it's true. You're unhappy, we all know it and now somebody has given you an out but you don't want to hear it.'

'An out?' Eric turned from the cocktail cabinet.

'Not an out from you,' she said, waving her cigarette in his direction.

'Shut up, Vera,' said Karen sharply.

'No I don't think I will.' Vera's eyes glittered with defiance.

Edward raised both hands in the air. 'Hang on. Just hang on. I'm missing something here.'

'You and me both,' said Eric, frowning. 'Are you girls having a bust up?'

Silence.

'A-ha,' said Edward gleefully, 'there *is* something going on. And I reckon it's to do with the Americans, or at least with Barbara.'

There was a subtle tightening of the atmosphere.

'One of you say something,' said Eric, moving back to sit on the sofa, an empty scotch tumbler in his hand.

'Go on, Vera,' mumbled Karen. 'You've started so you may as well finish.'

Vera looked from one brother to the other. 'Right.'

'The thing you've got to remember,' said Karen, cutting into the pause, 'is Barbara's coming from a place of love.'

'Yes, she's only trying to help.'

Vera and Karen locked eyes.

'Girls,' said Edward, 'enough with the suspense already! You've got our attention.'

'Karen?' said Eric, gently.

She nodded, still not entirely sure how the conversation had boiled down to this. It had slipped through her fingers so quickly and was now a real thing. She felt out of control, terrified and confusingly excited all at once. The thrill of possibility sparked up again and something that just days ago had made her feel ill, was now beginning to look like a gradually opening door. Was Barbara's suggestion really so monstrous?

'Yep, okay, well the thing is, Barbara came up with an idea she's heard about in the States.'

'We're not even certain it's illegal,' added Vera, hopefully.

'It is in America.'

'Yes, but maybe not everywhere.'

'What?' Eric abruptly stood up. 'You're making me nervous.'

Edward rubbed his hands together. 'Oh girls, this had better be good.'

Vera took a breath. 'Eric, you and Karen want a baby, right? And you can't have babies. But I can. So Barb said what if I had a baby instead? Because you see, I can carry a child. I'm good at that and I can carry a child for you.'

'What is this?' murmured Eric, sounding woozy and confused, 'do you want us to adopt your baby? I don't...'

'We're not talking about adoption. It would be your child. Yours and Karen's.'

'But that *is* adoption.'

'No Eric, because you'd be the father. I'd just be the carrier. The baby carrier if you like.'

'What?' muttered Eric, still struggling to make sense of what he was he was hearing.

Edward rose unsteadily to his feet and lifted his forefinger to silence the others. He glared down at his wife. His voice was low and dangerous. 'You and I need to have a conversation, Vera. I'm not having this.'

A small frown appeared between Vera's perfectly arched brows. 'It's not about you. It's about helping your brother.'

All the colour drained from Eric's face. Distractedly, he

raked his fingers through his hair and then brought his palms together as though in prayer.

'I don't know why you think plotting something behind my back is a good idea. And if I've got this right, you girls have cooked up some...some theory that I'm going to have a baby with you, Vera.'

Vera nodded, bright eyed. 'It could work, Eric.'

'No,' he held up his hand, 'it couldn't.' He stared at his wife. 'Karen?'

Helplessly, Karen raised her shoulders. 'I don't like the *thought* of it any more than you, but what if...somehow...if we look at the whole reason behind it...we could be parents.'

Edward suddenly erupted. 'Shut the fuck up! Nobody is going to sleep with my wife, except for *me*. I can't believe you're all sitting around talking about this like it's *nothing*.'

'We know it's not nothing,' said Vera quickly. 'It's serious shit.'

'Yes, it's serious shit that is never going to happen. Jesus Christ!' He swung round. 'Karen? Are you okay with your husband fucking my wife?'

Karen flinched. 'No, of course not.' She faltered, scarlet-faced. 'But it wouldn't be like that, Ed. It would be for love.'

'Eric?' Edward rounded on him. 'Say something! For the love of God, please tell me you're not party to this obscene suggestion?'

'Of course I'm not! This is the first I'm hearing about it.'

'I feel fucking sick. How could you, Vera?'

Vera sat up ramrod straight and put a supportive arm around her sister-in-law.

'I can do it because I love Karen. And because you love Eric. And because it's a gift I can give to these two incredible people who want to be parents and should be parents, but the universe is so shitty and mean sometimes, it makes it impossible. I like being pregnant. Remember when everyone said how serene and glowing I looked with the twins? You liked me being pregnant. A magnificent galleon under sail, you said. Carrying two babies was easy for me; carrying one is no sweat at all.'

For a moment, Edward's eyes softened. He seemed to be trying to gather his thoughts, perhaps remembering the beauty of motherhood that so suited his wife. And then he blinked and the dreamy expression shut down like a steel trap.

'Fine. So we'll have a baby. You and me. Not you and my brother.'

'Ed, please listen...'

'I've heard enough.' He grabbed Vera's elbow. 'No time to lose. Let's go.'

'Stop it!' Vera tried to shake him off, but Edward's tight fingers were locked on her arm. Roughly he pulled her to her feet and shoved her towards the door.'

Eric strode across the room and barred the way. 'Cool down, Ed. Take it easy.'

'Move!' Still gripping Vera's arm, Edward shoulder-barged his brother and reached for the doorknob.

'Let me go,' gasped Vera, stumbling through the remains of her sons' birthday party. 'This is stupid.'

Already on her feet, Karen lunged at them. Her voice was high and panicked. 'Ed, please let her go. Vera....'

Edward twisted around and all but spat in her face. 'Get out of my house. Both of you. You fucking scheming bastards.'

'Ed!' Eric tried again to block his path, but his brother knocked him aside. Unbalanced and full of alcohol, Eric staggered backwards and landed heavily on the floor.

'This is *my* wife,' snarled Edward, staring down at him with contempt. 'You've got your own. And if you want to fuck something other than that skinny, withered bitch, then good luck to you, but you're not touching Vera.'

He yanked open the door and pushed her into the hallway.

'Eric! Do something,' gasped Karen in horror as she saw her best friend being hauled up the stairs. As they reached the top, Vera turned her tear-streaked face down to the hallway where Karen stood, shivering with fright.

'It's okay,' she said shakily through the banister bars, 'I've got this, Karen.'

'Shut up,' snarled Edward and angrily shoved her towards the bedroom door.

TEN

After the slam, there was a terrible silence. Karen stood at the bottom of the stairs staring up into the void and then Eric was beside her, his fingertips on her shoulder.

'We should go,' he said close to her ear.

Karen shook her head. 'We can't leave Vera.'

Eric's chest rose as he sighed. 'Neither can we stay here.'

Karen shifted slightly and dislodged her husband's warm hand. 'I'm not going home and leaving Vera here with...this.'

'Edward is her husband.'

Karen frowned. 'So?'

Eric looked ashen and exhausted. 'So we can't interfere,' he paused, 'in their marriage.'

Karen put one foot on the bottom stair. 'I'm scared for her, I need to know she's alright.'

'Love,' Eric gently held her upper arm, 'it's none of our business.'

Karen hesitated.

'They won't thank us,' murmured Eric. 'They'd prefer us to forget about it; pretend it never happened. Besides, they are probably up there having a conversation, that's all. And let's face it, they've got a lot to discuss. As have we.'

It was Karen's turn to take a deep breath. The last few minutes had obliterated all thoughts of Eric's feelings and how he might react to what Vera and Karen had proposed.

'Yes. Of course. I'm sorry Eric.'

'Come on,' he said, handing her her coat from the banister post, 'let's go home.'

They walked up The Narrows in the crisp chill of an early autumn night. Bright beams shone through the windows of homes where families gathered, where people felt safe and loved and secure. Karen cast a glance back at Edward and Vera's house, standing out blackly against the twilit sky. The only lights showing were from the front room where they had all been chatting and drinking earlier. She thought about the birthday party mess on the floor and the awful darkness of the upstairs windows.

BACK IN THEIR OWN HOME, Karen and Eric sat either side of the kitchen table, in silence. After a moment or two, Eric scraped back his chair and took a bottle of scotch and two glasses from a cupboard. He poured them each a stiff measure.

Karen couldn't stop thinking about Mark and Paul and whether they had heard anything from earlier. There hadn't been a peep from either of them - but now a new sadness descended on Karen - perhaps they were used to it.

Eric rejoined her and they sat facing one another, each struggling with where to start.

Finally, Karen raised her head and looked her husband in the eye.

'I wish tonight hadn't happened,' she said. 'I should have put a stop to the way it all came out.'

'I'll be honest with you Karen, I really don't know what to think. About any of it.'

'I didn't know Ed was like that,' said Karen softly. 'I've never seen this side of him before. Have you?'

Eric stared down to the glass of whiskey in his hand. 'Not really.'

'Where the hell did it come from? Nobody's ever said anything before. Vera certainly hasn't.'

'Well she wouldn't, would she? It's not something you want the whole world to know about.'

'But we're friends. How could she have a husband who treats her so badly and not tell me?'

Eric raised his shoulders. 'She's a private person I guess.'

'Does he hurt the boys?'

'I don't know, love. I don't think so.'

Karen rubbed her hands up and down her arms. She felt shaken up and cold.

'We should do something.'

Eric shook his head. 'There's nothing we can do. It's between Edward and Vera.'

'This is wrong.' Karen stood up and moved to the kitchen

window. 'It can't be swept under the carpet. Vera was upset...she was crying. It wasn't what she wanted and he dragged her away.' She faced the room again and folded her arms. 'I hate him.'

Eric looked haggard. He'd aged ten years over a short couple of hours. 'I'm sorry he said those vile things about you.'

'I think that's the least of the horrific stuff he's done today.'

'It's totally uncool though. And I won't forget it.' He gave a low cough. 'And I want to know what you, Vera and Barbara Hasting meant. I've gotta tell you, I'm struggling to understand.'

'We don't have to revisit it tonight.'

'Yes we do.'

Karen leaned back against the sink, her arms still folded across her chest, her shoulders high; wary.

'Come on,' said Eric and drained his glass of scotch. 'Please explain.'

'O-kay,' said Karen and moved to sit back at the table. He let her take his hands and they sat on opposite sides, with their fingers loosely linked.

'It's like I said before. Barbara is only trying to help and honestly, when she came up with this idea, I freaked out. I really did and so did Vera. I know it's a shock for you to hear it like you did, but the more I think about it, the more it seems like some kind of possibility for us. And it's asking so much of you, I get that - and it's asking so much of Vera and of me.'

'And Edward,' said Eric quietly.

'Yes, and Edward.'

Eric leaned back and his fingers disentangled from Karen's. 'How could it ever work? No man is going to let his wife sleep with somebody else.'

'But let's just suppose for a moment that Edward was on board.'

'Never going to happen.'

'*Hypothetically*, if Edward was on board and allowed you to sleep with Vera,' she paused, 'how would you feel about it?'

Eric reddened. 'How the hell can I answer? If I say, 'yeah great, I'll have sex with Vera,' you'll think I want to and I fancy her. And how's that going to help us and our relationship?'

Karen gave a quick shake of her head. 'Come on, of course you like Vera. Who doesn't? And it's okay, because I know you wouldn't be cheating on me. It would be for us.'

'Jesus. You're making it sound so clinical.'

'Absolutely. It would have to be.'

Eric ran his hand over his face. 'I don't know, Karen. I really don't think I could perform on demand and it not mean anything. The whole idea is grotesque.'

'Eric,' said Karen firmly, 'this is so we can have a baby. It's so we can be a family and the baby will be ours. Well, half ours. And if anybody is going to be the baby's other half other than me, well then I want it to be Vera.'

Eric gazed at his wife. 'But love, it's not going to happen. Even if Vera agrees...'

'She does.'

'...and even if I agree, there's Edward to consider. I can't do that to my twin; I just can't.'

'Yes you can. Frankly, after tonight I don't care about Edward at all.'

'He's my brother,' said Eric flatly as though it were the end of the conversation.

'Yes,' said Karen, 'and I'm your wife.'

ELEVEN

J ust before bedtime, Karen rang Vera's house. There was
no reply.

Eric hadn't said very much more after their kitchen
table discussion. He'd taken himself off for a walk around the
block. He didn't invite Karen to join him and she didn't ask.

The whole thing was wretched and upsetting, and Karen
lay in bed worrying about Vera. It was shocking to consider
perhaps it wasn't the first time Edward had exploded like this
and Karen found herself thinking back to occasions when
Vera had been quieter than usual, wearing long sleeves,
drinking too much. Had there been signs Karen had missed?

She pushed Eric for answers when he finally got to bed.
Had Edward been a violent child, a troubled teenager, a
bully? It was all but impossible to think this was the same
person who had always presented as a charming, capable
man.

Eric offered scant assurances and Karen couldn't quite believe he was as totally unprepared as she had been. There must have been times over the years when Eric had wondered. Perhaps he'd tried to block them out.

'I feel like the world has tilted,' said Eric.

Karen could only grunt in agreement. The rosy glow of liquor had long gone, leaving a dull thudding headache in its wake. Her mind was filled with the evening's images and emotions.

And Eric was right. Things would never be the same again. How could they? Eric, Karen, Vera and Edward had all learned things that shocked them. Words had spilled out that could never be unsaid. Theirs was a new reality now.

AFTER ERIC LEFT for work the following morning, Karen hurried down the road to Vera and Edward's house. There was no answer to her knock on the front door. Of course, Vera would be at school dropping off the boys.

Still dithering on the doorstep, Karen heard the click of the garden gate and then Vera was walking towards her, ravishing in a checked hip hugger skirt and white poorboy sweater. Every inch the groomed and confident mum.

Neither of them said anything while Vera put the key in the lock and let them both into the house. They made their way to the kitchen.

'Coffee?' said Vera and waved Karen to a chair at the table.

'Thanks.'

There was a pause as Vera busied herself with the kettle.

Karen couldn't keep quiet any longer. 'Are you alright?'

Vera faced her with a bright smile. 'Fine.'

Karen's heart sank. 'Vera, you don't have to do this any more. Are you really okay?'

Vera's beautifully made-up eyes swam and she pressed her lips together, but didn't reply.

Karen jumped up and grabbed her in a tight embrace. 'I'm sorry. I'm so sorry I left you last night, honey.'

'Oh that,' mumbled Vera into Karen's shoulder. Her voice was tight and false. 'That was nothing.'

Knots of tears were stuck in Karen's throat. She held Vera a little tighter, while behind them, the kettle merrily built up a head of steam. Karen guided her to the kitchen table and made the coffee herself, while Vera sat quietly, gazing down to her lap.

'Talk to me,' said Karen softly. 'This wasn't the first time, was it?'

Vera shook her head. 'I'm so ashamed.' It was barely above a whisper.

'What have *you* got to be ashamed of?'

'It's just...we're meant to be the perfect couple.'

'Why though?'

'Why does he knock me about?'

'So he *has* hit you before. Oh Vera.'

Vera gave a small sad smile. 'I believe the term is *punch bag*.'

Karen stared at her in horror. 'I had no idea.'

'Nobody does. He's pretty good at it too and never where

it's visible.' Vera's head fell into her hands. 'He'd kill me if he knew I was telling you this.'

'So was last night the first time it happened in front of people?'

'Usually he waits 'till we're alone. I can't tell you the number of times I've been shaking with fear riding home from somewhere in a cab, knowing what would happen when we got there. And I'd never really understand what I'd done wrong until it was too late and he'd give me that look. I'd talked to another man, I'd worn the wrong dress, I'd said the wrong thing, I'd looked at him the wrong way. It was always something different.'

Karen's heart filled up with love for Vera. '*Why* didn't you tell me?'

'What could you have done? Nothing.'

'And now Eric knows as well...'

Vera shook her head. 'Eric would never say anything against his twin.'

Karen had to know. 'What about Mark and Paul? Does Edward ever...?'

'No. But they see things; hear things. It's not an easy house to grow up in. I try, you know, but once their dad is angry...'

Karen felt sick. 'This can't go on, Vera. You've got to leave him.'

'Ha,' said Vera bitterly, 'and go where?'

'You can come to our house for a start.'

'No I can't. Edward would be round there straight away and who knows what would happen then?'

'There's got to be somewhere you could go, *something* we could do.'

'But Karen, I have no money of my own. How would I support the children?'

There didn't seem to be anything to say to this and Karen could quite see Edward would never stand for Vera being at their place. Everything Vera was revealing made her willingness to broach the subject of Eric and Karen's baby the night before, even stranger and more unlikely than ever.

'Why,' started Karen and then stopped. Vera was so vulnerable now the harrowing secrets of her marriage were exposed. It seemed cruel to heap on more distress.

'Why what? It's okay, you can ask me anything.'

'I just can't quite understand why you seemed so keen to bring up the baby situation,' she said carefully, 'knowing how Edward would be bound to react.'

'Alcohol,' said Vera simply. 'I was drunk as a skunk. And you two were there so I felt relatively safe.'

'You didn't seem any more tipsy than the rest of us,' said Karen, shaking her head.

'Huh. Ed isn't the only one who hides things,' said Vera. 'I thought you knew how much I drink.'

'Not really. I've never thought about it much.'

'Oh Karen, I've become quite ingenious.'

Karen folded her arms, her brow wrinkling with a new concern. 'You drink by yourself?'

'All day. I'm so used to it now it doesn't even affect me. I'm numb most of the time. It helps.'

'Vera, please. There must be someone you can talk to - a professional...'

'A priest? I don't think so.'

'Yes a clergyman - or somebody else. There must be places...'

Vera reached for a pack of cigarettes and lit one before responding.

'I'm not ready yet, Kar. I'll do it when I'm stronger.'

'Well when will that be?' said Karen and instantly regretted it. 'Sorry,' she whispered.

There was a pause while Karen too took a cigarette from the open pack on the table. Vera slid her slim gold lighter across the table. 'I'll tell you one thing,' she said and flicked ash into the ashtray, 'I'm serious about the baby.'

'Vera, no!' gasped Karen. 'It can't happen - what about Ed?'

'Forget Edward for a moment. Is Eric game?'

Karen gulped.

Vera didn't wait for a reply. 'Are you?'

Caught off guard, Karen faltered.

'Because,' said Vera, 'I am. I want to do some good in my life. I want to help two people I care about and *this* is something I can offer.'

'But Vera,' said Karen anxiously, 'what about Edward?'

Vera extinguished her cigarette and stood up. 'What about him? It's my turn to do what I want with my body.'

'Well of course you should have that right, but we need to be realistic. If you do get pregnant, Edward will know.'

'Yes and he'll think it's his.'

Karen squashed down a rising panic. 'So what happens when you give the baby to us?'

'Okay, this is where it gets difficult.'

'*This* is where it gets difficult?' Karen almost laughed.

Vera nodded, poker faced. 'We couldn't do it straight away. I'd have the baby and keep him for a while - which makes sense because I'd be feeding. And then after a number of months it would finally be over with Edward.'

'I don't get it.'

'When the baby was old enough, I'd hand him over to you. At which point...'

'Vera, this is madness.'

'At which point, Edward would divorce me. And if he didn't, then I'd divorce him.'

'Stop!' It felt like the waters were closing over Karen's head. 'You're going round and round in circles, Vera. You just said you can't leave him because you have nowhere to go.'

'I have nowhere to go right now as we stand here, but give me a year or eighteen months and I know I'd be stronger. I'll move away, get a job...'

'You can't walk away from all this.' Karen waved her hand around the gleaming kitchen. 'What about the boys? What about *you*? And what do you mean, you'll divorce Edward? Do you know how difficult it is? What are the grounds?'

'He beats me up. He *rapes* me.'

'That's horrific and wrong, but it's not a crime; you can't get arrested for having sex with your wife.'

'And he cheats on me. I swear to you, he's truly a monster.'

This was new information for Karen. It took a second for her to digest it.

'You'd need proof though, wouldn't you?' she said, slowly, 'the beatings would be so hard to prove, as would infidelity.'

'I don't know how to prove anything and at this point I don't care. All I can see is a window of opportunity where I can do something kind and decent for you and Eric. I know it will give me strength. I've achieved nothing in my life, Karen.'

It was Karen's turn to flare. 'You have two healthy children. That's an incredible achievement, don't talk about it like it's nothing.'

The two women faced one another.

'I think you want to do this whole thing to punish Edward,' said Karen finally. 'It's about getting your own back for a miserable marriage.'

'Oh my God.' Vera slumped onto a chair and gazed up at her. 'No, Karen. It's not about getting something over on Ed. I want to have a baby for you and Eric, and I'll tell you why. First and foremost, I want to help you be a mother. If that sounds bizarre or trite then I'm sorry, but it's true. I also want to leave my husband, but as we know, I'll be in dire straits financially and every other way, if I up sticks and do it now. I can't do it to my boys. So I'm making a plan. A plan to leave when the new baby is old enough. I'll have done what I set out to do and not had to worry about money or a place to live. You'll have the baby and the boys and I will go. I don't know if you can understand this, but this gives me time to squirrel housekeeping money away and really make a solid plan.'

Karen stared at her aghast. 'You're not listening to me! Your life would be ruined.'

Vera gazed back, clear-eyed and assured. 'No Karen, it wouldn't. My life would be my own, and I'd finally be able to breathe.'

TWELVE

Eric phoned Karen from the office and asked to meet her for a drink after work. They did this sometimes and often went to the cinema afterwards or out for dinner. Karen jumped at the chance to sit down with him and talk, away from the house where an atmosphere of growing unease made meaningful conversation almost impossible. It felt like the whole neighbourhood had taken on a wary veneer. Even the street seemed to be holding its breath.

Karen walked past Vera and Edward's house on the way to the train station, glancing over the facade as she did so. All seemed quiet and the low afternoon sun made mirrors of the windows. She thought about Vera being alone in the house all day, secretly drinking and dreading her husband's return from work. Karen almost abandoned her plans with Eric to go and tap on Vera's door, but knew she had to sort out her own marriage before she could hope to help anybody else.

When she arrived at the bar, Eric was there, sitting at a table near the back. He had already ordered a round of drinks.

'Hello love,' he said and stood up to give her a kiss.

'Hi.' Karen settled at the table and picked up her port and lemon. 'Cheers.'

They tapped glasses.

Karen jumped straight in. 'Did you see Edward at work today?'

'No, he was out. Dot said he had client meetings.'

'All day?'

'Apparently.'

There was a pause.

'Have you seen Vera?' said Eric eventually.

Karen shook her head. 'Not today, but we had a long chat the day after the party. I've been wanting to talk to you about it, but it's never felt like a good time to broach the subject.'

'Right.'

'Yeah, look Eric I have to know, are you really a hundred percent against the baby idea?'

Eric blanched. 'There it is,' he murmured.

'I've gone over it and over it a thousand times and after talking with Vera, I know she's willing - more than willing - to help us, but obviously it all depends on how you feel.'

'What about Edward?'

Karen sighed. 'It's bad, Eric. He's a wife-beater for God's sake.'

The colour drained from Eric's face. He spun a quick look around the bar. 'That's an outrageous thing to say.'

'It's true, and he cheats on Vera as well.'

Eric took a sip of beer.

'I see,' said Karen, studying him from across the table, 'you're not surprised. How long have you been aware?'

'I don't know.'

'He's your twin, of course you know. One way or the other - you know. So, how long has it been going on?'

The battle for Eric's loyalty was playing out across his features. He looked in torment.

'Since Mark and Paul were born. Maybe before, I couldn't really say.'

'Who has Edward been with?'

Eric couldn't look at her.

'You know what, it doesn't matter who it is,' said Karen. 'I'm guessing people from work or clients or whatever.'

'Anna,' he whispered and lowered his head.

'What? The babysitter? She's like *twelve* or something. God Almighty.'

Eric shrank deeper into himself. 'It's a relatively new thing with her, but there have been other women over the years.' He dragged his eyes to Karen's face. 'Vera knows?'

'She knows he cheats,' said Karen, 'but I don't think she knows about Anna. She'd never let that happen - Anna wouldn't even be working there if Vera suspected anything.' Karen gathered herself. 'Why have you let this go on? If you knew your brother was having sex with a teenager, why didn't you put a stop to it? And don't say it's because he's your twin and you love him. He's a vile, disgusting man who assaults women and preys on young girls.'

'What do you want me to do? Report him to the police for infidelity? Edward isn't breaking any laws - Anna's not underage. And anyway, it's none of my business.'

Karen's mouth fell open. 'Well it should be.'

Eric burred up. 'He knows what I think and he doesn't care. We've had plenty of fights about it, believe me.'

'How can you stand being around him at work every day?'

'He's not a bad person. He's not. You know Ed, most of the time he's a top bloke. He looks after Vera and the boys - they want for nothing.'

'Yes, except to be treated with love and respect. I can't believe you're defending someone who's so self-obsessed and callous he thinks he can terrorise his wife and bang the fucking babysitter!'

'Karen!'

'Stop sticking up for him, then!'

'You can't go round calling him a wife-beater. He cheats, yes but he'd never hurt Vera. Come on, have you ever seen so much as a mark on her?'

A hot spike of rage exploded deep in Karen's gut. 'He rapes her,' she spat. 'You saw him force her up the stairs the other night and then you said they were probably going to *have a conversation*. He's clever and cruel and makes sure he only leaves marks where Vera can hide them. Wake up, Eric! Your brother is dangerous as far as women are concerned. And one of these days, his boys will catch him in the wrong mood and bam! They'll be next.'

Eric picked up his beer and put it down again. He ran an

agitated hand over his face. 'I didn't know he was hurting Vera,' he muttered. 'I know he has a temper and can be a bit rough round the edges, but not this.'

'You didn't want to see it,' countered Karen. 'You're blinkered when it comes to your brother, but I'm telling you, the more I hear about Edward, the worse it gets. He doesn't deserve your love and loyalty.'

'I'm just glad Mum and Dad aren't around to see this,' he said, shaking his head. 'They'll be turning in their graves.'

Karen sipped her drink. 'Vera's going to leave him,' she said quietly.

Eric's head came up. 'Is she?'

'She's making a plan and it'll happen over the next year or so. Her unhappiness and - let's face it - fear, are driving her desire to have the baby. She is deadly serious Eric and wants to do this for us while she still has the means to support her boys financially. When the baby's born, she'll nurse him for a few months and then she'll take her twins and go. We'll have the baby then.'

Eric stared at her. 'It'll kill Edward if she takes off.'

'No it won't. It'll damage his ego, but he'll survive. And frankly, I don't care about Ed at all. My concern is for Vera and the kids and what he'd do if he caught up with them.'

'What about the baby?'

'He'll think it's his, so we can expect all hell to break loose.' Karen faced her husband squarely, 'and he'll never forgive you. Ever. If we go ahead with the baby, you'll have to accept you won't have a brother any more.'

Eric studied her, his eyes filled with anguish. 'When did you get to be so hard, Karen?'

Her reply was swift and heartfelt. 'When I saw Vera being dragged up the stairs like a terrified animal. When I found out he beats her. When you told me about Anna. When I saw the man for who he really is.'

'I need him though, he's my family,' said Eric softly.

'No Eric. *I'm* your family. Vera and her boys are your family, and our baby - he'll be your family. You don't have to be part of Edward's twisted sickness for a single second longer. Make the decision, cut the ties and let's give ourselves the life we want. If I can stand by and know you're intimate with Vera and still be able to love you both, then you can, too. If you need a family as much as you say you do, then here's your chance. It's up to you now.'

THIRTEEN

Huge, important decisions were teetering on the cusp of three people's moral compass. It nearly killed Karen to keep quiet, but she wisely opted not to bombard Eric with her need for an answer. In the meantime, she conferred with Vera and they agreed, albeit with very few words, that they were both fully committed to the plan. It made Karen feel queasy to think about the logistics, so she stuck with what she could handle for now. *Do you want to have a baby? Yes. Are you willing to do what it takes? Yes.*

Two nights later, as Karen began to clear the dinner table, Eric stirred.

'I've been thinking.'

Halfway to the kitchen, Karen froze. Gently she placed the dishes she was carrying on the sideboard, and rejoined him.

'Okay,' she said cautiously and clasped her hands in her lap to stop them from shaking.

'Once this thing is done,' said Eric in an unfamiliar, low monotone, 'I never want it mentioned again. When it happens, don't ask me for details. If it has to happen more than once, don't get suspicious or jealous or crazy.' Eric didn't have to say what *it* was.

Karen could hardly breathe. 'So you'll do it?'

He nodded.

'Thank you. Thank you so much, Eric.'

A small furrow creased his brow and he gave a brief shake of his head. 'Sort out a time and place with Vera,' he said gruffly, 'the three of us should talk first.'

'Okay.' Karen was certain her husband could hear her pounding heartbeat. 'Thank you.'

'Don't say that.' He looked at her, sitting flushed and anxious on the opposite side of the table. 'And don't get emotional.'

'Yes. Okay. Sorry.'

Eric pushed back his chair and stood, gazing down at her. 'We're all going to hell for this, you know.'

'No we're not,' retorted Karen sharply. 'This is a beautiful thing - we're giving life to a new little person. Vera can reclaim her power and you and I will be blessed with a baby.'

'We're making a mockery of my brother's life,' said Eric flatly. 'We're not just liars, we're cheaters, deceivers and manipulators. There's no place in heaven for people like us.'

'Yes there is,' whispered Karen, as he walked out of the room and closed the door.

∽

THEY MET in secret the following Thursday morning. The days leading up to it were the longest of Karen's life. Every time the phone rang she thought it was one of the others changing their mind.

She picked an anonymous cafe on Guildford High Street, close enough to home and far enough from central London and the office. It was busy with midmorning shoppers when she pushed open the heavy glass door and went in.

Vera was already there, reading a magazine at a scarlet Formica-topped table in the corner. It was hideously awkward and Karen slipped into the seat opposite her without a word.

A second ticked by and then another.

'Hi,' said Karen eventually.

'Hi.' Vera closed the magazine and dropped it on the seat. 'Alright?'

'I think so. You?'

There was a pause.

'Is Eric coming?' said Vera.

'As far as I know. We didn't discuss it this morning.'

'Far out, this is creepy.' Vera winced. 'I feel like I'm having an affair with both of you.'

Karen gave a tight, unhappy smile.

'Here he is.' Vera sat up a little straighter as Eric stood near the door, scanning the cafe.

Karen raised her hand in a little wave and he made his way over, sharp in his suit and lace-up Oxfords.

He took a seat next to Karen and a waitress bustled up, notepad in hand to take their coffee orders. It broke the moment, forced all three to speak and Karen felt a slight loosening of tension.

'Thanks for coming,' she said to her husband.

'Sure.'

'So,' said Vera, looking at the couple in front of her, 'what's the plan?'

Karen risked a glance at Eric's face. 'We need to make sure we're all a hundred percent on board,' she said.

'We're here, aren't we?' said Eric.

'Yes. Okay well then the next thing is to...'

'Pick a day,' said Vera succinctly.

'Jesus.' The colour drained from Karen's face, but Eric was nodding.

'Yes, and a place I suppose.'

'My house,' said Vera without hesitation. 'In the afternoon. Karen, you can collect the boys from school and take them to the park or something.'

'What?' Karen's hand drifted to her mouth.

'Well you don't want to be there, do you?' Vera looked up as the coffees arrived. 'Ta.'

'Far out,' muttered Karen, 'of course not.'

'Afternoons work, because Eric you'll go to the office as usual and then make an excuse to duck out early. It would make sense for you to have some sort of appointment on your way home.'

'Dot looks after our diaries,' said Eric quickly. 'She'd know...'

'Make something up,' retorted Vera.

Karen stared at her, appalled and weirdly impressed at

how detached she seemed. She picked up her coffee for something to do.

'Alright then,' said Vera, lighting a cigarette, 'one day next week. Tuesday's good.'

The bitter espresso burned Karen's lips. 'Good in what way?'

Vera blew smoke into the air. 'My cycle.'

'Oh.' Karen felt like an idiot. This was excruciating.

'Tuesday afternoon, then,' said Eric and stood, his untouched coffee cooling quickly on the table. He bent down and brushed his lips against Karen's cheek. 'I'll see you at home.'

She couldn't look at him.

'Bye Vera.'

Vera gave a curt nod and drew on her cigarette again.

Eric dropped a pound note on the red Formica for the coffees, and then walked straight-backed through the cafe and out of the door, the shop bell clanging in his wake.

FOURTEEN

Tuesday arrived and Karen woke up to grey October rain trickling down the bedroom windows. She rolled over, but Eric had gone. She lay quietly with a hammering heart as her sly destructive mind led her down the sickening path of wondering how Eric would prepare for this day, which suit he would pick, which aftershave, which underwear.

She pulled herself out of bed and left the bedroom, down the carpeted stairs, and into the kitchen.

The radio was on. The Beatles were singing. Eric was making breakfast. Karen noticed his shirt, blindingly white in the gloomy autumn morning. His narrow tie and neat hair. She watched his hands as he buttered his toast.

Eric looked up and saw her leaning against the doorframe in her pyjamas. He tried to smile and she did too, but it simply wasn't going to wash. With a sigh, Karen levered herself upright and went to him. He put down the butter knife and held her close. They didn't say anything.

A few minutes later, he left for work.

TIME DRAGGED. Karen had a bath, got dressed, tried to eat something. She thought about phoning Vera or going to see her, but backed out at the last minute. What was there to say, after all? Instead she kicked around the house all morning, unable to settle.

Mark and Paul's school was a fifteen-minute walk from The Narrows. Karen got there early and joined a gathering of mums waiting outside. She kept an eye on the time, her mind constantly straying to Vera's house and what was happening there. She cast covert glances at the other women, some with prams, some with bored toddlers. They all seemed to know one another and sent small, interested smiles Karen's way. What would they say, she wondered, if she strolled up and announced, 'my husband is having sex with my sister-in-law in her house, right now. They're actively trying to make a baby. They're in bed and I'm here. Funny old life, isn't it?' Instead she smiled politely back at them. 'Thank goodness the rain stopped before the kiddies come out.' They murmured in agreement.

The school bell made Karen jump and then the civilized chitchat of suburban mums was shattered by hollering children bolting out of school, unbuttoned mackintoshes flying, socks dribbling down sturdy calves.

'Auntie Karen!' Paul came hurtling towards her with Mark in hot pursuit.

'Hello boys,' she cried. They crashed into her with their strong little limbs and muddy shoes. They smelled of the classroom and wet grass.

'Where's Mummy?'

'Mummy's a little bit busy this afternoon, so she asked me to come and pick you up.'

'What's she doing?' Mark looked confused. Their mother was always there to collect them.

'We're going to the park,' said Karen with a bright smile. She caught the eye of Mrs. Parkinson, the teacher and gave her a friendly wave, then held out her hands to the boys. 'Let's go.'

Suitably distracted, the twins latched on and she led them out of the school gates and down the road as they skipped along by her side, chattering.

Vera had said to bring them home at 4.00pm. Karen sat on a bench at the park as the light faded from an already drab afternoon. Mark and Paul scrambled tirelessly over the climbing frame and went up and down the slide at full tilt. Karen hoped they wouldn't start asking when they could go home for tea. She knew how quickly things could deteriorate once the twins realised they were hungry, it was getting cold and they wanted their mum, but for now they were running on the special kind of adrenalin that comes from an unexpected trip to the playground with their favourite auntie on a school day.

Karen checked her watch. It was 3.30pm. She looked up and saw Vera walking across the grass.

Paul spotted her from the top of the slide.

'Mummy!' he yelled, waving madly.

Mark scampered over from the roundabout and Karen watched as Vera knelt on the damp grass with her arms around him, waiting for Paul to finish his go on the slide. Then she scooped her children close and kissed the tops of their heads.

Karen got unsteadily to her feet, watching it all unfold from her spot at the bench. Her face was rigid as she tried to read Vera's body language from twenty paces. A stab of frustration pricked her insides; it took a mammoth effort to patiently wait until the family reunion was over. Finally the boys disentangled themselves and ran back to the play equipment.

'Five more minutes,' called Vera and then walked over to the bench, collected and expressionless and sat down, gesturing for Karen to do the same.

'Everything alright?' Karen's voice came out in a feeble croak.

Vera shook her head. 'I'm sorry.'

Karen's pulse quickened. 'Sorry for what?'

'Nothing happened. I'm really sorry, Karen.'

'Did Eric turn up?'

'Yes he arrived right on time, but when it got to the point of...' She stopped. 'When it came to it, he didn't want to - well, couldn't - go through with it.'

Karen gaped at her. 'What happened?'

'Well - nothing.' Vera raised her shoulders.

'I don't understand. Tell me everything, from the beginning.'

'Karen love, I'm not going to do that.'

'Yes! You must.'

Vera checked the twins, who were playing tag, ducking and weaving around the swing set. It was nearly dark.

She sighed. 'Like I said, he showed up.'

'What were you wearing?'

Vera flinched. 'What?'

'What were you wearing? I want to know.'

'Jesus.'

'Tell me.'

'A...a negligee.'

'What colour?'

'Karen, please.'

'What colour?'

Vera cleared her throat. 'Black.'

Karen nodded emphatically. 'So you answered the door in the middle of the afternoon in black lingerie?'

'Well, I had a robe on, too.'

'And then what?'

'I offered Eric a drink.'

'Had you already had one?'

Vera gave her an old-fashioned look. 'Of course I had.'

'Did he drink anything?'

'No.'

'Okay, so then what? Did you go upstairs?'

Vera dropped her head. 'This is horrible,' she muttered. 'Don't torture yourself like this Karen.'

There was a pause, heavy with expectation.

'Fine,' said Vera. 'Yes, we went to the bedroom and I kissed him.'

'Did you kiss him or did he kiss you?'

'I started it. I put my arms around his neck and kissed him.'

'On the mouth?'

Vera nodded.

Karen's hand rose to her lips. 'Then what?'

'Well, we were kissing and then I undid his belt.'

'Uh huh.' Karen squeezed her eyes shut. 'Yep, go on.'

'And I thought he was, you know, ready...'

Silence.

'So,' said Vera hesitantly, 'I sort of took his hand and led him to the bed. I lay down and he lay down next to me.'

'Did he touch you?'

'Yes.'

'Intimately?'

'Yes.'

Karen pressed her palms to her already closed eyes as though trying to block out the images she was so determined to see.

'And then,' said Vera, sounding stronger, 'Eric sort of stopped and got off the bed. He said he was sorry but he couldn't go on any further. And that was it.'

Karen released the breath she'd been holding and her hands fell into her lap.

'Thank you for telling me,' she whispered.

Vera was silent. She sat watching her twins for a few seconds and then got to her feet and called them over.

'I'll see you soon,' she said to Karen as the boys arrived, out of puff and disheveled. Then she took each of them by the hand and they walked over the darkening grass, through the park and home.

FIFTEEN

Two weeks passed and nobody mentioned the events at Vera's house. Karen didn't feel she could ask and neither Eric nor Vera brought it up.

It was there, though. A shadowy presence hanging over Karen and pressing down on her relationships with the other two. She felt trapped under the weight of everything unsaid.

Life on The Narrows went on as before but one Wednesday morning when Karen and Vera were shopping in London, Karen finally blurted out what she'd been dying to ask.

'Are you going to try again with Eric?'

She saw Vera's fingers tighten on the hanger of a pink gingham dress. There was a small silence.

'Let's go for lunch somewhere,' she said quietly.

'Okay.' Karen paused, 'are you going to buy that?'

Vera put the dress back on the rail. 'It's sweet, but I'll leave it for now.'

They walked through Selfridges and didn't speak again until they were outside on Oxford Street. Vera glanced around for a cafe.

'Over there?'

Karen shrugged. She sensed something in Vera. Apprehension maybe. Possibly even dread.

They made their way across the street, settled at a window table and placed their order for lunch. Karen wasn't even hungry. She was certain Vera was pulling the plug on the baby plan.

'Look,' she said 'I know Eric didn't fulfill his part of the bargain, but I really hope you won't give up.'

Vera reached up and smoothed her hair. 'It's not working, Karen.'

A band of tension tightened across Karen's forehead. 'Please, don't abandon it because nothing happened that time. In a way, I'm happy to think it was so impossible for Eric to sleep with you, even given the circumstances. It makes me feel loved. I'm sure he just had cold feet because it was all so strange and forced. If you would just try again. I'll talk to him - it'll be okay, just please don't give up.'

Vera gazed at her. 'The afternoon at my house wasn't the only time.' She opened her handbag and took out a pack of cigarettes.

'Pardon?' Karen felt like snatching the packet away.

'There have been other times, too.'

Karen's mouth was a hard, tight line. She didn't trust herself to speak.

Vera lit the cigarette and rested her elbow on the table. 'We tried again. Twice.'

'Tried again when?'

'The next day.'

'Where?'

'A hotel.'

'Oh my God.'

'And the day after that.'

'Why didn't you tell me?'

Vera glanced out of the window. 'Eric didn't want you to know. I think part of the reason he felt so awkward and embarrassed at my house is because you knew what was happening. It freaked him out.'

Karen's brain was spinning; a kaleidoscope of images, none of them good.

'You went to a hotel twice and had sex with my husband behind my back. Wow.'

'Hey, hang on a minute,' said Vera quickly. 'This is for you, remember?'

'Is it?' said Karen, 'or are you beginning to enjoy it? A guilt-free extramarital affair with no strings. Hell, it's not even a problem if you get pregnant!'

'It's not like that. You're being paranoid now.'

'Did being on neutral ground do the trick? Did he at least get it up this time?'

'Don't do this, honey,' murmured Vera, 'it's not a joke.'

'Did he? And believe me, I'm not joking.'

Vera sighed. 'No. It was the same as the time at my house.'

'Jesus, what's wrong with him?'

'He *loves* you, Karen. He still sees it as cheating and he just can't do it.'

Needles of frustration ran up the back of Karen's neck. 'What's the answer then?'

Vera pressed her lips together.

'Ah,' said Karen slowly, 'I get it. You and Eric have discussed this. Come on then, tell me.'

'He said he couldn't do it unless you're there.'

'I can't get pregnant though, that's the whole point. If I could have a baby, we wouldn't even be having this conversation.'

Vera fixed her with a hard stare. 'He wants you there.'

'What, to *watch*?'

'No...to...take part.'

Karen's stomach lurched. 'He wants a friggin' threesome?' She leaned back, with her arms tightly crossed over her ribcage. 'He's having a bloody laugh.'

Vera looked at her, stony faced. 'Eric said he needs you there.'

The blood rushed back into Karen's face. 'So he and I will make a start and then you jump in at the last minute? Seal the deal kind of thing? That's disgusting.'

'Look,' snapped Vera leaning over the table, 'do you want a baby or not? You said you'd do anything, so fucking get on board. I love the way you're sitting there like a bloody nun, making judgments and calling the shots when it's me and

Eric who are doing everything we can to help you. Pull your-self together Karen, or I'm out.'

Hot tears sprang into Karen's eyes and she furiously blinked them back. The whole situation was alien and scary. And what Vera had said was true; she and Eric were doing all the work while Karen stood idly by and minded the kids. Or that's how it seemed. She glanced at Vera, beautiful, generous Vera whose own life was filled with miserable secrets, yet who still found it within herself to do something so outside the norms of morality it was almost absurd. And for what end? To make a child for somebody else.

Karen dropped her head, ashamed.

SIXTEEN

Eric was already at the hotel when Vera and Karen arrived. He sat in the lobby, calmly reading the paper. The moment she saw him, Karen started to shake. It felt like they were about to commit a crime. At any second, Vera would whip a gun out of her handbag, wave it around and scream at everyone to hit the floor.

As they approached, the kitten heels on Karen's shoes made little clacking sounds. The tap-tap of Vera's stilettos sounded bold; in control. Karen could see a hotel key and a white plastic fob sitting on the coffee table in front of Eric. She ran her tongue quickly over her dry lips. This was really happening.

He nodded at them, but nobody could manage a hello smile. Eric folded the paper and stood, scooping up the key as he did so and dropping it into his jacket pocket. He led the way over to the lifts. Karen was certain every single person in the hotel knew what was about to happen. Vera caught her eye.

'It's okay,' she whispered, 'everyone probably thinks we're prostitutes.'

Karen let out a bark of horrified laughter. Eric frowned over his shoulder and mortified, she gave a brief shake of her head. Vera raised her eyebrows as though flummoxed as to what was funny and Eric turned back to the shiny lift doors in front of them. Karen felt a bead of sweat gather on her top lip.

There was a polite ping as the lift arrived and the trio stood aside as people exited and spilled into the foyer. Eric let the ladies in first and then the three of them stood awkwardly towards the back and waited for the doors to close.

Karen watched the numbers light up in the few seconds it took for them to reach the third floor of the hotel. The lift came to a halt with a soft bump and then the doors were opening again.

Eric became businesslike, striding down the corridor with the key now in his hand. Karen suddenly wondered if this was the same hotel he and Vera had visited before. He seemed to know where he was going.

They stopped outside a cream painted door, adorned with a gold number 26. Karen glanced up and down the carpeted corridor. The identical doors lining each side weren't giving up their secrets. There was nobody else about; it was lunchtime on an unremarkable October day.

Inside the room, the curtains were partly drawn,

shrouding everything in half-light. The bed looked enormous. Eric immediately went to the mini bar and started pulling out miniature bottles of alcohol. Vera sat daintily on the only armchair in the room while Karen hovered near the door.

'Here,' said Eric and held out a glass to his wife.

'What is it?'

'Gin.'

Eric passed a glass to Vera, too. She shrugged and knocked it back without comment. Karen stared at her gin for a while and then held her breath and downed it in one. With no ice, lemon or tonic, it tasted like medicine and she shuddered. Eric emptied a measure of scotch into a teacup and drank it swiftly. He shrugged out of his jacket, undid his tie and sat down on the end of the bed. Karen watched him with a kind of strange fascination, as though she'd never seen her husband undress before.

Vera cleared her throat, a jarring intrusion in the shadowy room. 'Karen,' she said and inclined her head to where Eric waited. He held out his hands.

Karen placed her empty glass on the bedside table and went to him, slipping out of her shoes as she crossed the carpet. Gently she parted his knees and stood between them, then cradled his head against her chest. Eric's hands went to her waist and they stood there for a moment or two in silence.

Vera rose. 'You guys have got to relax,' she said with quiet authority. 'I'm going to the bathroom.' She moved to the en suite and closed the sliding door. Karen heard the hum of the fan, and the perceived distance Vera had afforded them gave her courage.

She ran her fingers through Eric's thick dark hair and leaned down to whisper in his ear.

'This is our chance, darling. We have to give it a shot.'

He looked up at her, his eyes full of something she couldn't decipher. 'I know.'

Karen gave him a gentle push and he lay back on the crisp white bedcover. She confidently held his gaze as she stepped out of her clothes and went to lie beside him on the bed. She rested her head on his chest, one arm draped over him in an old familiar way.

Eric's heart thumped loud and fast against her ear.

'It's okay to be nervous,' she said softly. 'I'm scared too, but please know I love you, I trust you and I can never thank you enough.'

He sighed then and the tension left his body. 'My beautiful girl. I want so much to have a family with you.'

Slowly Karen began to unbutton his shirt, leaving feathery kisses down his chest as she went. He closed his eyes and Karen sensed a ripple of static run through his body. She brushed her lips across his mouth, and heard the catch in his breath as she lowered herself down to sit astride him. Unhurried, deft, his fingertips rose and traced her neck, her jawline, the contours of her face. It had been so long since they'd been close like this. Karen felt a swell of desire so sharp she gasped.

There was a movement from somewhere beyond them and then Karen caught the sensuous notes of Vera's perfume.

Something exploded deep in her gut. Maybe fear, maybe lust, she didn't really know. And then Vera was there too, her hair hanging long and loose and soft over the pale, perfect skin of her shoulders. She reached out and ran her forefinger down Karen's cheek and smiled deeply into her eyes.

'It's okay,' she said and Karen felt a huge sob of gratitude rise up. This wasn't the soulless, sordid sex she'd feared; this was beautiful, selfless love. She willingly moved aside and went into to the bathroom, where she sat on the floor with her arms around her knees and prayed to whoever would listen. Please let there be a baby.

SEVENTEEN
HEATHROW AIRPORT, LONDON
PRESENT DAY

Cathy saw Andrew first and immediately wished she hadn't.

She'd decided at some point on the 14-hour flight that to see him first would be preferable, as then she wouldn't be caught unawares. It was important to be on the front foot, but the tedious trawl through passport control, the striding down corridors, the queuing and waiting and hanging around had worn her down to the point where she just wanted the actual meeting bit over with. And now she was thinking how much easier it would be, to have him approach her instead, tap her on the shoulder and say 'hey, long time no see!' There'd be no time to be nervous.

But of course, that didn't happen.

She zeroed in on him the moment she emerged from customs; fancy four-wheel-drive suitcase as light as a feather spinning along behind her like a shiny-backed puppy, handbag sensibly slung across her body, a bottle of duty-free wine dangling from her free hand in its gaudy plastic bag.

Look at me. Be the first to say hello.

Andrew scanned the crowd, directly over Cathy's head so she was obliged to walk right up to him.

'Hey,' she said, without looking at his face. 'Long time no see.'

'Cathy!' He grabbed her shoulders.

'Hello,' she mumbled into his dark red jumper.

He stepped back to study her properly. 'Look at you!'

'Dear God, please don't.'

She ran a quick hand through her hair and raised her chin to meet his smile.

'Okay?' he said.

'Just tired.'

'Righty-o, let's get you home. Shower and change, glass of wine, bite to eat and you'll be sorted.' He took Cathy's suitcase out of her grasp. 'Car's this way.'

Travel stained and exhausted, Cathy followed across the crowded concourse and as Andrew weaved through the melee of Arrivals, she luxuriated in being able to watch him, unobserved. He'd always been on the tall side, but now the curly hair was greying, the stubble was rougher, the long fingers were stronger. The boy now a man, with a lifetime of stories of which she knew nothing. And here he was, laughing over his shoulder as he strode towards the lifts, dragging her suitcase, leading her home. The best friend she hadn't seen for over three decades. Her safe place and wingman, her confidante and buddy. Her cousin, Andy.

'I'M SO sorry about your dad,' said Cathy as they weaved through rows of vehicles in the car park. He was always lovely to us kids.'

'Thanks Cuz. It's an awful thing to say and - you know, probably a bit crass - but it was a blessing in the end.' A sleek silver Audi beeped as they approached and the boot lid rose. 'This is us. Hop in the front.'

Cathy slid into the passenger seat while Andy loaded her bags in the back. The car smelled new and expensive. She shivered in the flat metallic air, so different from California.

They navigated their way out of the car park, pulled into crawling traffic and waited at a set of lights while overhead, lumbering planes flew deafeningly low as they came in to land.

'So Uncle Eric - he'd been ill for a while?' said Cathy.

'About two years. Well, maybe longer but that's when he was diagnosed.' Andy manoeuvred around an illegally parked car. 'Lung cancer,' he added, shaking his head. 'It was so sad but you know, he wouldn't listen. Mum tried her best, but he was chain smoking right up to the end.'

Cathy looked out of the window. The London Borough of Hounslow stared back at her.

'So, how're things with you?' said Andy. 'You left England - and then what happened?'

'Ha,' said Cathy with a grin, 'let's see, a lifetime's worth in...how long have we got?'

Andy glanced at her. 'You haven't been back at all?'

She shook her head.

There was a pause. 'Have you visited the States?' she said.

'I've been to New York a couple of times with work, but you were in San Francisco by then and the meetings schedule was crazy. I'd have loved the chance to see a bit of the country.'

'And your favourite cousin?'

He laughed easily. 'Of course.'

Cathy leaned back in her seat. 'Thirty-odd years.'

'Well,' said Andy, as he accelerated onto the motorway, 'we've got lots of time for catching up. I want to hear everything.'

She closed her eyes, smiling. 'Me too.'

'Good idea - have a nap. It can take nearly an hour sometimes, depending on the traffic.'

Cathy sat up. 'I thought you lived in town.'

Andy grinned. 'I do, but we're going to Mum and Dad's now. Give yourself a day or so in the burbs to get over the jet lag, and then come up to Soho. Mum's expecting you - the spare room is all ready. She'll have made dinner too, probably.'

'How kind,' murmured Cathy, 'I didn't mean to put her to any trouble.'

'No trouble,' said Andy cheerfully, 'to be honest, it's given her something to do. She's looking forward to seeing you, so prepare to be fussed over.'

'How's Auntie Dot doing?' said Cathy, 'after - you know, your dad and everything.'

'Mum's stronger than she looks. Stoic little thing, she battles on, bless her.'

'What will happen now, with the house and so on?'

'Early days. We haven't talked about it yet, but once we've had the reading of the will...'

'Yes,' said Cathy, 'of course, when is that?'

'The day after tomorrow at Dad's solicitor's in Guildford.'

Cathy dropped her head. 'It was so weird to get their email,' she said quietly. 'I thought it was spam; nearly deleted it.'

Andy sent her a quick sidelong glance. 'He loved you. He really did.'

She nodded. 'He was a lovely uncle - a real gentleman.'

The mood dropped for a second.

Andy pulled into the outside lane and overtook a green van advertising gardening services.

'How are your folks?' he said, easing off the accelerator.

Cathy's chin puckered. 'Dad - well, you know. I never see him. Last I heard he was living at the beach with a forty-something-year-old.'

'Do you miss him?'

'God no, I never think about him to be honest.'

'What about Auntie Vera?' said Andy carefully.

'Ah, Mum. By all accounts she's doing alright. "As well as can be expected" as they say.'

'Do you get updates from the nursing home?'

'Occasionally. And you know, she doesn't need anything.'

'Except to see you, I guess.'

Cathy bristled slightly. 'And now I'm here.'

'Indeed you are,' Andy reached over and touched her hand, 'and I'm so glad.'

THE AUDI TURNED into The Narrows and Cathy took a giant step back in time. First impressions showed her a street basically unchanged since she left. Her own home was around the first corner. Her eyes slid over it as they drove sedately past and her pulse quickened. She didn't comment and neither did Andy.

'Here we are,' he announced unnecessarily and pulled into the short driveway of his childhood home a few doors down.

Cathy studied the front of the house through the windscreen; a dark brick and tile Englishman's castle, which seemed smaller than she remembered. It hit her that this visit was strange and confusing on more than one level. She needed to pull herself together. Andy was switching off the engine and his mother, Cathy's newly widowed aunt and now sole occupant of the house, was already on the doorstep.

Cathy took a deep breath, and got out.

EIGHTEEN

Auntie Dot had everything under control. The house, decorated in quiet blues and creams was immaculate. The sitting room mantelpiece was loaded with sympathy cards. Dinner was ready.

The three of them sat around a polished wood dining table. From Cathy's seat, she could see a china cabinet to the left of the kitchen door and a bookcase to the right, exactly as she remembered it. The pendant light hung over the table of pink flowery dinnerware. The tablecloth and napkins matched.

Andrew's mother hurried in and out of the kitchen; a small elderly lady neat as a pin, her face a blotchy red from weeks of crying. Cathy suspected she would never recover from Eric's death.

They settled down to eat and then Dot took a breath. 'Would you say grace please Andrew?'

Cathy put down her knife and fork, slightly embarrassed at not remembering the family routine. She bowed her head while Andy murmured reverently.

'Auntie Dot,' said Cathy softly when the meal resumed, 'I'm so sorry about Uncle Eric.'

Dot's pale eyes filled immediately. 'Thank you, dear.'

'He was a wonderful man.'

'Yes, he was.'

Andrew passed a tureen of vegetables to his mother, and she spooned beans onto her plate with a pinched, worried look. Cathy focused on her dinner and kept quiet, wondering what was coming.

'How is Edward?' said Dot eventually.

Ah. The evil twin.

'I don't see Dad these days,' said Cathy honestly. 'The last I heard he was living on the coast.'

'In your part of America?'

'California, yes. Los Angeles.'

'Right,' said Dot, sounding more confident, 'I had a feeling you lived there too.'

'Cathy's in the Napa Valley, Mum,' said Andy. 'It's quite a long way from Los Angeles.'

'I see. And the boys?'

'They're doing great,' said Cathy. 'Mark's working in New York now. He's an anesthesiologist in a big teaching hospital there and Marie's a teacher.'

Dot frowned, remembering. 'I don't think I know his wife...'

'No, Auntie they met in the US a long time ago.'

'Any children?'

'Yep. Twins, actually. Petra and Louise.'

Dot nodded. 'Yes, now you say it, I think I recall hearing something about Mark's daughters. What about Paul?'

Cathy paused with the fork halfway to her mouth. 'He and Candice live in Canada.'

'Heavens,' said Dot, 'what's he doing there?'

Cathy suppressed a smile. 'Candice is from Toronto and all her family are there, so...'

Dot nodded, implying this made perfect sense to her. 'Family is so important,' she said firmly. 'At the end of the day, it's all we have.'

'Glass of wine, Cathy?' said Andrew.

She met his eyes, grateful for the diversion. 'I'd love one.' It was hard not to feel the sting, the veiled criticism from Dot that Cathy really had nothing to do with her family. That she lived quite happily in another country with very little care for her father and no care whatsoever for her poor mother, languishing away in a nursing home in Tunbridge Wells.

After dinner, Dot shooed Andrew and Cathy into the conservatory, insisting they leave the dishes and she'd make them a coffee.

'Let her,' said Andy under his breath as Cathy hesitated, 'she wants to keep busy.'

They wandered into a large glass conservatory, a late addition to the house, Cathy thought. From her comfortable wicker chair she could make out the stone terrace and steps leading down to the lawn. Night was gathering and she felt full and sleepy.

'I remember playing cricket out there,' she said. 'All of us kids. I was always outnumbered, being the only girl.'

'You did alright.'

Cathy smiled sadly. 'It was so much nicer at your house than my house. I think I drove Dot and Eric round the bend because they could never get rid of me.'

'They loved having you here.'

'Did they? I used to have the feeling Dot really wanted you and Eric to herself.'

'Rubbish.'

'Maybe.' Cathy sighed. Home had been an unpredictable jumble of lavish attention and blazing rows, of tiptoeing around her father's explosive temper and feeling the ground shake as he slammed every door on his way out. And after each outburst, hearing her mother's quiet sobbing from behind the bedroom door. It was a house of fear and trying to do the right thing. She'd always felt she was basically on her own. Her brothers showed little emotion and the three of them never discussed it. Andy's house was a soft place to land.

Cathy wasn't sure if it was the overwhelming tiredness that comes from sitting on a plane for hours and hours, or whether it was the rosy glow from her memories of Andrew's home, but she felt herself relaxing; her guard was down.

'Do you ever hear anything about Auntie Karen?' she asked quietly.

Andy looked at her across a glass-topped coffee table. The windows behind him were almost completely black. He shook his head.

Cathy pressed a little further.

'I don't remember her at all,' she said, 'but I know she did a disappearing act. Nobody ever explained anything to children back then.'

'All I can tell you,' said Andrew, 'is she left The Narrows. No-one has ever told me anything, either.'

'She'd be...what...mid-eighties now?'

'I suppose so.' Andy tilted his head to one side. 'Why are you asking?'

'I don't know really. I guess I'm trying to piece this family together.'

There was a pause.

'Will you go to see your mother?' Andy's voice was kind, but the question still prickled.

'Of course. I said I would.'

'Yeah, but...'

'Vera's an old lady too now. How can I feel,' Cathy looked up to the ceiling; sighed, 'resentment and anger for things that happened years ago?'

'She would have had her reasons.'

Cathy shrugged. 'She preferred the bottle to her children, that's all I know.'

'Here we are,' said Dot brightly as she entered the conservatory holding a tray of cups and saucers. Andrew leapt to his feet.

'It's alright, dear,' said his mother mildly, 'I can manage.' She placed the tray on the table with a clatter. 'What are you two gossiping about?'

Cathy gave a short laugh. 'The past, I guess.'

Dot handed her a cup of instant coffee. 'No point doing that, is there? Things are often best left where they belong.'

'You're probably right, Auntie.' It seemed futile to pursue her questions about Karen, although Dot would probably know everything from back then. Cathy glanced at her aunt, old and vulnerable, broken hearted from the death of her husband and desperately trying to cover up how scared she might be to face the future alone.

They drank their coffee in silence and then Andrew put his cup back on the tray and stood.

'I'd better get the car back.'

Cathy stared at him. 'The Audi? I thought it was yours.'

'God no, I can't afford that. And there's nowhere to park at the flat, anyway. Plus, you really don't need a car in Central London.'

'Whose is it then?'

'Ah you know, one of those keyless hire jobs. I'll drop it back at the designated spot in Westminster.'

Dot caught Cathy's eye. 'It's all very modern,' she said conspiratorially. 'Whoever heard of a keyless car?'

Cathy smiled.

NINETEEN

Two days later, Cathy, Andrew and Dot sat in the waiting room of the solicitor's office in Guildford. The appointment was the reason behind Cathy's visit to England; the reading of Eric's will.

If Dot was surprised at Cathy's inclusion, she didn't show it.

'You were always his favourite of Edward's children,' she said and that seemed to be enough.

Cathy wondered if her uncle had felt sorry for her, growing up. Clearly unhappy at home, she had spent as much time as possible with Andrew. Her twin brothers were a few years older, and at least they had each other. Cathy and Andrew were best friends. Andy understood her, he was fun and straightforward and kind in a world where kindness was in short supply. Vera's moods were dependent on how much she'd had to drink that day. Sometimes Cathy was showered with affection; Vera would stroke her face and hold her and cry into her hair. Sad, drunken tears which Cathy didn't understand. Mark and Paul would be off somewhere with their friends, or playing sport or disappearing into Twin World where their kid sister wasn't welcome. Life at Andrew's house was calm and orderly. Dot was gentle; Uncle Eric was benevolent. It felt safe there.

None of this could have prepared Cathy for what was to happen, though. When Frank Green, the solicitor read the contents of the will she felt punched in the solar plexus.

Uncle Eric had left her a cool million pounds.

It didn't sink in. Cathy sat on the hard wooden chair between Andrew and Dot, feeling faint. Frank Green continued reading. One and a half million for Andrew and the house, stocks and shares to Dot, to the value of two million pounds.

Dot gasped.

'I had no idea,' she mumbled through splayed fingers. 'I knew he was good with money...I...we never went without, did we Andrew? But this is a fortune.'

Andrew sat very still. His clasped hands were in his lap.

Frank Green continued speaking in his measured lawyer's tone, but Cathy had tuned him out. She watched his serious face and square-rimmed glasses, took in his suit and blue shirt, tie and matching pocket square, his pale hands with a signet ring on the little finger, his expensive watch.

A million pounds.

And then Frank Green was standing up and leaning over the desk to shake hands with them all. First Dot, then

Andrew. Cathy found her voice and thanked him, then followed the others out of the office, back through the waiting room and onto the pavement.

THE UBER DROPPED Dot at home and then Cathy and Andrew continued on to the city. Neither of them said very much in the car. The Uber driver's name was Nigel. His RAV4 was squeaky clean; he offered his passengers bottles of water. He'd been doing this gig for a month, he said.

Cathy was glad to be sitting in the back, where she could zone out from the niceties while attempting to process what had transpired at Frank Green's office, and Andrew was uncharacteristically subdued, answering Nigel's enthusiastic chitchat as succinctly as possible.

They arrived at Andy's flat in Soho and got out in a flurry of polite thanks and good-luck-with-the ubering. Nigel looked pleased with himself and drove off towards Tottenham Court Road.

'Home sweet home.' Andy indicated the four-storey terraced building in front of them, with an extravagant sweep of his hand. Downstairs was a shop. Cathy caught a glimpse of cool street wear in the window, which, on closer inspection had no price tags.

'This way,' said Andrew affectionately, pulling her towards a bottle green door to one side. He swiped the keycard and went to take Cathy's suitcase, but she waved him away and followed, trudging up a narrow set of stairs to the first floor level, with her case in her arms. There was a tiny square landing and another door, which opened onto a light, airy space all bare floorboards, scatter rugs and tall windows.

'Okay,' said Andrew, dumping his backpack on the ground, 'Quick tour.'

'Living room, kitchen through there,' he marched across the room and threw open another door, 'bedroom and bathroom. I'll sleep on the sofa, so you're in here.' He stood aside and Cathy entered a fresh navy and white bedroom.

'I can't kick you out of your bed,' she protested.

'Yes you can, it's done. Unpack your stuff and have a shower or whatever. We can go out to eat if you like? Actually, it's probably best if we do; there's nothing in the fridge.'

'Sounds good, but I'm buying dinner.'

'Fine, we can argue about it later.' He backed out of the room and closed the door with a soft click.

Cathy sat on the end of the bed, still reeling from the contents of Eric's will. Her brain was mush. A million quid - *over* a million dollars. She didn't deserve this incredible kindness, and how did Dot and Andrew feel about it? A stab of guilt for all the things she'd never done for her family pricked her conscience.

She resolved to go and see her mother the following day.

THEY WENT to eat at a spectacular alfresco food and dining mall down the road from Andy's place. The UK summer was lingering into September and people were making the most of it; the precinct courtyard was studded with trees and packed with tables of noisy chatter. Cathy felt herself loosening up.

They found a relatively quiet spot outside an Indian restaurant and ordered a bottle of wine. Cathy leaned back and observed Andrew on home turf.

'This place is magical,' she said as thousands of fairy lights came on in the twilight, lacing the trees with strings of white stars.

'I love it here,' said Andy and held up his glass. 'Cheers. And welcome back to London.'

Cathy took a sip of velvety red wine.

'Very nice.'

'Ah ha,' he said, 'I'm glad the expert is impressed. Come on then, where's it from? Just the country will do - and no cheating.' He slid the bottle out of her reach.

'Expert,' scoffed Cathy, 'as if. Working for a vineyard doesn't mean I know much about wine. I like what I like.'

Andrew folded his arms. 'Which country?'

Cathy grinned. 'Fine.' She took in the wine's bouquet and then tasted it, allowing the wine to stay in her mouth for a moment before swallowing.

'Australia.'

'Yes! Very good. Can you pinpoint where?'

'South Australia does a lot of excellent shiraz.'

Andrew nodded. 'Go on.'

'The Barossa Valley?'

'Bravo!' Andy pushed the bottle back towards her. 'We'd better finish it, I reckon.'

She laughed easily. Being with Andrew was the most natural thing in the world, but something was troubling Cathy; an insistent little voice in her head. She looked her cousin in the eye.

'There's an elephant we need to discuss.'

Andy raised his eyebrows. 'Is there?'

'Come on,' insisted Cathy, 'we can't skirt round it forever. Did you know what was in your father's will?'

'No, and neither did my mother. Dad was old school. You didn't discuss financial matters with anyone, not even your wife and definitely not your child.'

'Look Andy, I have to know - are you okay with Uncle Eric leaving me this money? It's so much. I've gotta tell you, I feel awkward.'

'Well don't. It's clearly what he wanted.'

'Don't get me wrong, I'm incredibly thankful - but I don't understand.'

'Listen Cuz, just accept it. You had a rough old time growing up - we all saw it - but you never lost your sweetness in all the chaos of home. And I know you don't really believe it, but mum and dad loved having you around. You were the daughter they never had.'

Cathy stared into his kind brown eyes, so much softer and deeper than his mother's anxious pale blue. 'You look like your dad,' she murmured.

'Do I? Maybe.' His gaze dropped and he picked up his glass.

NENE DAVIES

Cathy felt a twist of something deep inside. It hadn't gone away, this connection with Andrew. She felt as close to him now as she had years ago. It was surreal to be sitting here in this fairyland in London. They were both in their fifties, but she felt young and energised; the years were melting away. She put down her wine.

'We should eat something,' she said quietly.

'Yes ma'am.'

TWENTY

They walked back to Andy's apartment a little the worse for wear. They had indeed finished the bottle and ended up drinking another one, followed by a nightcap. Cathy braced against the sharp night air and Andrew draped his arm around her shoulders.

'How about a mug of warm milk?' he said, reminding her of Dot's remedy for a wakeful child.

Cathy gagged. 'Jesus. I hated it then, and I hate it now. Tepid, full cream...'

Andrew gave a soft chuckle. 'Poor mum, she tried her best and you were always too polite to say no.'

'Let me tell you,' said Cathy firmly, 'it was heaven to be offered something as homely as milk at bedtime. At my house you'd like as not get a clip round the ear.'

Andrew glanced down at her. 'Was your dad really that bad?'

'Worse. He should never have been a father. He wanted mum all to himself, but she got more and more addicted to alcohol and wasn't there for anybody; him or us. He was an angry, angry man.'

'I don't remember there ever being a nanny or babysitter...?'

'Ha! Not after mum found out dad was sleeping with half the neighbourhood.'

'Really? My folks never said anything.'

'Who really knows? Mark and Paul told me one day when I was about ten, I think. Apparently there was an unholy row over a babysitter when they were little, but whether or not it's true is anybody's guess.'

They stopped outside the flat.

'Alright, no hot milk then. Vodka it is.'

Cathy rolled her eyes. 'A small one. I'm dead beat.'

Upstairs, they sat on the sofa and clinked their shot glasses together.

'Thanks for having me,' said Cathy. 'I still feel guilty about sleeping in your bed.'

'Don't. It's fine.'

'Have you got a partner?' She waved her glass around the room in a vague sweep, 'a wife and kids hidden away somewhere?'

'I do have a partner, yes. Sammy.'

Cathy pulled up. She hadn't expected this. For some reason she'd assumed Andrew was single; everything about him suggested he was, right down to his flat, which showed no sign of another person.

'Well, where is the mysterious Sammy then?'

'Touring.'

She prodded him. '*Touring*? How about a bit more?'

Andy shrugged, 'not much more to say. When your partner is a workaholic...'

'What sort of work, though?'

'Dancing.'

'What, like ballet dancing?'

'No, Sammy dances in shows.'

'A showgirl!'

Andrew laughed. 'Stage shows.'

'Ah, hence the touring. When's she back?'

'He. Sammy's a bloke. And he'll be back in town on Saturday.'

'I didn't know you were gay.'

'How could you?' said Andy kindly. 'Hell, we haven't seen each other since forever. And I'm bi, actually. There have been a few girlfriends over the years, too, but no children. I'm sad about that actually, I think I'd be a good dad.'

'Tell me about Sammy. How did you guys meet?'

'At work.'

'Actually, yes - I haven't even asked what you do.'

'I'm a choreographer.'

Cathy slapped his arm. 'Jeez, another thing I never knew. Good on you - seriously, that's fantastic.'

'I love it,' said Andy 'and being around energetic fit people keeps me young. I can't imagine any other life, really.' He paused, 'but what's your story? Husband, wife, children?'

'Nope.'

'Never?'

Cathy gave a rueful smile. 'Well yes, if you want to go back through the mists of time, I guess I was married once.'

'You were?'

'Yeah, not too long after I arrived in New York. It was the 1980s and here I was, a fresh-faced English girl, all bangles, loud make-up and dressed in neon from head to foot.' She grimaced.

'Alright,' said Andy, 'let's start from there. How did you land up in America?'

'Dad took me. Mark and Paul had already flown - or should I say fled - the nest.'

Andrew put his drink on the floor. 'And all this time I was stuck in boarding school and lost track of everything. Why did Vera stay in England?'

'She got left behind, she didn't stay through choice.'

'And that's when your parents divorced?'

'Yes, but my father had dragged it out for years. No wonder poor Mum ended up a basket case.'

'I don't understand though. Why did your dad hate your mum so much?'

Cathy shrugged. 'She drank; I guess she was a liability. Who really knows what goes on in a marriage?'

'Okay, backtrack a bit. You and your father went to New York. Why America?'

'Dad knew some people from way back. A fat-cat client who used to own a cigarette company. My dad and your dad worked for him years ago. This guy, Larry Hasting sold the company when it was at its peak and made a fortune.'

'Hasting Cigarettes?'

Cathy sipped her vodka. 'Yeah. It was super famous; up there with the big brands.'

'Yes, I've heard of it.'

'Our dads worked on their campaigns in the sixties and early seventies. Rumour has it, they helped turn that whole company from a well-known American brand, to a global phenomena. You must have heard stories over the years?'

Andrew sighed. 'I didn't think about my father's work life much. Maybe kids aren't too interested in what their parents do and Mum never talked about the past. She still doesn't.'

'Not like my dad,' said Cathy, 'he bragged his ass off about the Hasting account and loved being associated with the family, so of course I was a major let-down when my marriage failed.'

'How so?'

'OK, well Barbara and Larry Hasting have a son, called Larry.'

'That's original.'

'Larry *Junior*.'

'And you married him?' Andy's eyes were wide. 'When you got to New York? You must have been pretty young.'

'Young, stupid and broke. Broke because I was trying to further my education on minimum wage and stupid because I wouldn't swallow my pride and ask Dad for the money.'

'Well what happened with the marriage?'

Cathy spread her hands. 'It was a complete disaster. If it hadn't been for Junior's mother Barb, who was actually a really gracious, beautiful woman, I couldn't have stood it for as long as I did. You see, my father and Junior's father wanted nothing more than to put us together and like I said, I was naive and foolish - and flattered too I guess. But the deal involved securing the family line.'

Andy's eyebrows rose.

'Babies,' said Cathy, 'I was supposed to have children to keep the Hasting name going. And the problem was, I couldn't conceive.'

'I was going to ask you about kids...'

'I didn't have a hope. Endometriosis, stage four. God, the pain.' Cathy shivered. 'I tried everything available back then but nothing worked and I ended up having a hysterectomy.'

Andrew gave a slow shake of his head. 'That would've been so tough. And all this time I was away. I couldn't believe it when I came home for Christmas and you'd gone. Just pfft - disappeared.'

Cathy frowned slightly. 'What did your parents say?'

'That you and Uncle Edward followed your brothers to America and Auntie Vera was still living on The Narrows. It was the strangest time. She basically locked herself in the house; became a recluse really.'

'Poor thing,' said Cathy sadly, 'nobody treated her very well, did they? Myself included. Do you know, when Dad bundled me off for this shiny new life in the Big Apple, I barely looked back.' She paused. 'I hated that house.'

TWENTY-ONE

According to Google, Honeysuckle Lodge Nursing Home was located thirty miles south east of central London, in Royal Tunbridge Wells, Kent.

'Hmm,' said Andrew over Cathy's shoulder, 'The Garden of England. Very nice.'

'I'm going to visit my mother. Come with me?'

Andrew handed her a takeaway coffee. 'I don't know. Do you think she'll remember me?'

'I don't know if she'll even remember *me*,' said Cathy, 'but if you're free this morning, I'd love your company.'

Andrew hesitated, his head on one side.

'Alright,' he said, 'why not?'

Cathy breathed out. 'Thank you. I feel quite nervous.'

Andy walked around the sofa and sat down next to her.

'Nervous about seeing your mum?'

'I don't know how she'll react, how she'll feel about me turning up.'

'Do you think she knows you're here? Maybe it'd be better to call first; let the nursing home know you're coming.'

'I emailed them last week before leaving California,' said Cathy, 'and the head of nursing messaged back, saying it was okay to visit any time. They have an open door policy apparently.'

'Did they give you any idea about your mum's state of health?'

Cathy shook her head. 'Physically she's quite well I believe, but I don't know what to expect.'

'She must be up to seeing people though,' said Andy reasonably, 'otherwise they'd have told you.'

'I guess.'

'We could go by train,' said Andrew, 'but it's a bit of a schlep. Taxi's going to be more than double the cost, though.'

Cathy grinned at him. 'Didn't we both just inherit a million pounds? I say we blow the expense and get another Audi on loan.'

'God, I'd forgotten,' said Andrew. 'How stupid.' He paused, reddening, 'wow, what kind of ungrateful son am I?'

Cathy ran a supportive hand down his arm. 'It's okay,' she said kindly, 'I think it's nice you're not focused on the money.'

'Dad was always so careful. Not tight-fisted, but measured - cautious. You know?'

'Unflappable,' said Cathy, 'and nobody's fool. So different from his twin brother. I think my father has a screw loose. He had so much, yet it was never enough.'

Silence fell in the small square living room. Early morning London sunshine filtered through the sheer white curtains leaving squares of light on the wooden floor. It was peaceful here, calm.

'Alright,' said Andrew after a moment or two, 'let's go and see Vera.'

THEY CHATTED in the car the whole way to Kent.

'So,' said Cathy, 'Sammy's coming home tomorrow - does he live with you?'

'No, he has his own place.'

'Is it serious?'

Andy laughed. 'You sound worried, Mum!'

'No Son, just interested.'

Andrew's eyes softened. 'He's a lovely guy.'

'But?'

'Ah look I'm not sure. He's a fair bit younger than me so there could be a time when I'm too old and decrepit for him.'

'I think you're in love.'

Andy grinned, unabashed. 'I am! But I always do this - fall madly in love and ruin everything by being too intense. This time, I'm trying to play it cool.'

'Hence the separate flats.'

'Yeah.'

'Well,' said Cathy, 'I can't wait to meet him.'

'And you?' said Andrew, 'anybody waiting for you back in the Napa Valley?'

'No, I'm a proud single lady. Have been for years, now.'

'Don't you get lonely though?'

Cathy shrugged. 'I adore my job. It's full on and I'm with people every day so I value being alone. But lonely? No.'

Andrew gave her a sidelong glance. 'Yeah, keep telling yourself that.'

She let it slide and looked out of the window.

'Work,' said Andrew, 'tell me about that.'

Cathy tucked a stray lock of hair behind her ear.

'I'm a brand manager.'

'Which is?'

'I champion a portfolio of brands in the marketplace.'

Andy gave a snort. 'You sound like a job advert. What do you actually do?'

'I work for a winery and do exactly what the ad says,' she said, grinning. 'I market a variety of wines and run functions, too. We have a bunch of upscale clients and do launches, parties; all kinds of social events. It's awesome to work with so many creative people. Keeps me young, much like your Sammy keeps you young.'

'What's the Napa Valley like?'

'Hmm, well it has a kind of Mediterranean climate with mountain ranges all around...'

'As the word *valley* implies,' interrupted Andrew.

She fixed him with a stern look. 'And the weather conditions, plus the geology of the place make it ideal for growing wine grapes.'

Andy gazed at her.

'Come back here,' he said earnestly, 'London's a really

great city. There's nothing for you in the Napa Valley that you can't have right here in good old Blighty.'

'You did hear me use the words *Mediterranean climate*, didn't you?' Cathy gave him a shove. 'Jeez.'

They found Honeysuckle Lodge easily enough, just off the main road about two miles out from Tunbridge Wells itself. A solid, white painted building which could have been a rectory in a former life, the home was set down a short drive-way. Andy and Cathy turned in, their wheels crunching over neat brown gravel. Flower borders and a high wall shielded the house from the main road and directly in front of the imposing black front door was a small lawned area, where three wrought-iron benches were arranged around a fountain which wasn't working.

Cathy cast about for a car park and spotted a hand-painted wooden sign with an arrow, indicating they should drive around the back. They left the Audi under a beech tree, next to a minibus emblazoned with the home's logo. Three or four other vehicles were parked nearby. It was very quiet.

'We should probably go back to the front door,' whispered Cathy.

'What?' Andrew slammed the car door.

'Shush!'

Andy shrugged. 'Come on,' he said briskly and set off.

Cathy didn't move. She looked up at the back of the house and a mass of windows and mismatched eaves and chimney pots stared back at her. Vera was in there - possibly even looking out of her window at this very moment and wondering who they were.

She heard Andrew's footsteps coming back.

'Okay?'

Cathy took a breath. 'Do I look alright?'

Andy's face softened. He held out his hand. 'You look lovely.'

They walked down the side of the house and approached the front door. Cathy reached up and rang the bell.

TWENTY-TWO

Head of nursing, Helen Peterson greeted Cathy and Andrew and ushered them into an office to the right of the front door. In the few steps it took to get there, Cathy sensed the warmth and cleanliness of the place. She glimpsed a vase of flowers on a side table a little further down the hallway. There was no stale smell of dinner, or bleach, or worse. It was like walking into somebody's much loved, freshly spring-cleaned house which, she realised, was exactly what it was.

Helen Peterson settled Andy and Cathy on one side of a desk, which was loaded with paperwork and a large computer. Thank-you cards with pictures of flowers and kittens were pinned on the wall behind Helen's head along with a clutch of newspaper cuttings and photos, some faded with time. Certificates in frames were lined up above the corkboard.

A woman who looked to be in her mid-forties was working at another desk. Her string of wooden beads exactly matched the colours on the pattern of her long-sleeved dress. Her fingers, skimming over the keyboard were full of silver rings.

'This is Monica Jackson,' said Helen by way of introduction, 'our office manager and paperwork guru. We'd be lost without her.' She gave a soft chuckle.

Monica Jackson glanced up and pushed her glasses onto the bridge of her nose. She smiled and gave the visitors a small wave.

Cathy sat opposite Helen Peterson, her mind brimming with questions. She had never stopped to really consider Vera's day-to-day life. The woman in front of her now was clearly a key figure, who would have up to the minute information about Vera, her health and state of mind. It made the moment very real and even a little shocking. Cathy felt Andrew shift in his chair and wondered what he was thinking.

Helen's dark blue uniform rustled as she leaned on the desk and interlocked her fingers, inching the wireless keyboard out of the way, to make room for her elbows. There was a file alongside the computer, which Cathy presumed to be her mother's. She felt a rush of shame for not engaging more over the years; Vera's primary caregivers should not be strangers to her daughter.

'How was your flight?' asked Helen politely, glancing from Cathy to Andrew.

'Oh this is my cousin, Andrew. He's based in London.'

'I didn't know Vera had extended family living so close - it's nice to meet you.' Helen's tone was pleasant, but Cathy felt another stab of guilt. 'My flight was fine, thank you,' she added belatedly.

'Alright,' said Helen, becoming businesslike, 'I expect you'd like a bit of an update.'

'Yes please.'

'First though, can we get you both a cup of coffee? It's nearly time for elevenses.'

The old-fashioned term warmed Cathy's heart. 'That would be lovely.'

Monica Jackson pushed back her chair, having seemingly been listening in. 'I'll be right back,' she said brightly and walked out, closing the office door quietly behind her.

'So,' said Helen, 'your mother.'

Cathy cleared her throat.

'When is the last time you had any contact?' Helen's chestnut eyes looked straight into Cathy's, but there was no judgment there. It was simply a question.

'I haven't seen Mum for over thirty years.' It sounded so cold and unloving. Cathy winced. 'I only heard she was here at Honeysuckle Lodge about six years ago. Up until then I believe she was still living in the family home.'

'Yes, sounds about right,' said Helen and clicked open a folder on the computer screen.

'My father emailed with her change of address one Christmas,' added Cathy.

'I see.'

'Do you know the circumstances?' said Cathy. 'Was she sick? Was she referred here from a hospital?'

'Actually, no,' replied Helen mildly. 'She chose us herself.'

Cathy opened her mouth and closed it again. Vera had to be reasonably robust to make big decisions like that.

'So she's pretty healthy, then?'

'Ms. Douglas...'

'Cathy.'

Helen's head dipped. 'Cathy. Your mother is quite unwell, I'm afraid. She's an alcoholic and in the early stages of dementia.'

Cathy swallowed. 'Okay,' she said slowly and felt Andrew's supportive hand on her elbow. 'And has this come on recently? The dementia I mean.'

'It's hard to say. If a resident has trouble with balance, or they're slurring - or displaying antisocial behaviour, it's sometimes difficult to know the cause.'

Cathy's brow puckered. 'But she can't be drinking in here, surely?'

Helen spread her hands. 'There are two schools of thought. On the one hand, if residents are physically able to get themselves to an off-licence or pub or if somebody brings bottles in for them, there is little we can do. It's their choice, after all. The other view of course, is to deny access at all costs. Both options have a downside, as I'm sure you can imagine.'

'So which one is Vera?'

Cathy looked up at Andrew's question.

'Vera does have alcohol in her room,' replied Helen,

'although sometimes she forgets where it is and can get quite upset if she thinks somebody has taken it.'

Cathy leaned back, absorbing everything she was being told. 'Does she walk into Tunbridge Wells to buy it? It's a good couple of miles.'

'We have regular outings in the minibus,' said Helen, 'and Vera is always first in line. Your mother is quite a character.' She smiled kindly. 'Let's go and see her. Monica will bring your coffee to Vera's room, but first we need to get you signed in.'

They left the office and walked down the corridor. A staff member in a pink and black uniform hurried down the stairs, smiling at the trio as she disappeared into one of the rooms. A clatter of teacups and chatter bloomed out of an open door on their left and Cathy glimpsed a spacious room where residents were seated in comfortable armchairs. A young carer in pale blue pushed a man in a wheelchair over to the window. Another staff member was bending over a drinks trolley. 'Two sugars for you Doreen?'

Helen stopped outside an open door. 'Here we are,' she said and gave a light tap as she entered the room.

Cathy's heart was in her mouth. She hitched her bag on her shoulder and followed.

An overabundance of floral patterns made the room seem cluttered. The bedspread and curtains matched and a thriving dark pink orchid in a white pot sat on the windowsill. The television was on and an elderly lady was sitting in an easy chair, with the newspaper across her knees. Her head drooped and she appeared to be asleep.

Helen discreetly turned off the TV and squatted next to the chair. 'Vera,' she said softly, 'you have visitors.'

The others waited just inside the door. The room was stiflingly hot.

Helen glanced back and beckoned Cathy over.

TWENTY-THREE

Vera looked up. Her eyes, a watery grey were deep in their sockets. Her mouth, a crazy-paved mass of lines. The formerly lustrous up-do a wispy birds nest.

Cathy knelt next to her. 'Hello Mum.' She put her hand over Vera's resting on the newspaper.

Vera drew back, confused. She stared at Helen for confirmation.

'Isn't it lovely,' said Helen encouragingly, 'Cathy's here. We told you your daughter was coming all the way from America to see you.'

Ever the hostess, Vera made a monumental effort. She delicately withdrew her hand from Cathy's and smoothed down her hair.

'Hello,' she said.

'Andrew's here too,' said Cathy and shuffled forwards to make room. Andy leaned down and brushed his lips across the paper-thin skin of Vera's cheek. She gazed at him in silence.

'You can sit here,' said Helen and Cathy saw a second chair had been pulled up on the other side of Vera. Andrew got stiffly to his feet and perched on the end of the bed.

'Alright,' said Helen cheerfully, 'I'll leave you to chat with your family, Vera. Elevenses are on their way.'

Vera's eyes followed Helen all the way to the door. Cathy licked her parched lips.

'How are you Mum?' she said, turning again to the old lady. 'It's me, Cathy.' She touched her chest with her fingers.

'I can see that. You haven't changed at all,' said Vera.

Cathy released a breath. Unexpected tears burned behind her eyes. She blinked.

'Neither have you,' she whispered, resisting the temptation to reach up and smooth a brittle strand of hair from Vera's forehead.

'Nonsense,' said Vera firmly. 'I'm an old crock and you know it.'

Cathy squeezed her hand.

'They didn't tell me you were coming,' continued Vera crossly, 'or I'd have changed my dress.'

'You look beautiful.'

Vera grunted. 'You haven't lost your accent, at least,' she said and then broke into a fit of coughing.

Cathy glanced at Andrew in alarm. He got up and went to retrieve a glass of water from the bedside table, but Vera waved an impatient hand.

'Fetch my cigarettes,' she wheezed.

'Oh Mum, I don't think you're allowed to smoke in here.'

'Take me outside then.'

'Hello,' sang a friendly voice and a staff member appeared in the doorway with a drinks trolley. 'Coffee time!'

'I'll take it in the courtyard,' said Vera.

'It's quite raw out there today,' said the carer, 'better to stay in your nice cosy room.' She began handing out the drinks and put a plate of biscuits on the side table.

'What a fuss,' muttered Vera peevishly and shook her head.

'Thank you,' said Cathy to the woman. She smiled and left the room.

'They make a decent cuppa in here at least,' said Vera and sipped her coffee, having seemingly forgotten about the cigarettes.

'Bickie, Auntie Vera?' Andrew held out the plate.

She took one. 'You two as well,' she said, 'eat up.'

The three of them sat in silence for a moment and then Vera addressed her daughter.

'What brings you all the way from America, then?'

Cathy put down her coffee and brushed her fingertips together.

'Well Mum, I'm sorry to tell you that Uncle Eric has died.'

'Died?'

Cathy nodded, watching her mother's face closely.

'Hmmm.' Vera stared into space. 'What did he die of?'

'Lung cancer,' said Andrew quietly.

'Ah.' Vera wrinkled her nose. 'Poor old Dot,' she said, 'she won't cope, you know. I'd better go and see her.'

'Mum's doing quite well,' said Andy. 'She likes to keep busy.'

'Oh she always did,' said Vera, 'busy busy busy - and she absolutely doted on the twins.'

Cathy bit her lip, uncertain which set of twins Vera was referring to.

'Do you ever hear from Mark and Paul?' she said cautiously.

'No. Do you?'

Cathy shook her head. *Please don't ask me about dad.*

'And Edward? Any news of him?'

'Sorry Mum, Dad and I aren't in touch, these days.'

'What a family,' muttered Vera in disgust.

Cathy could only agree.

VERA ACCEPTED Andrew and Cathy's goodbye pecks on the cheek with cool detachment but when Cathy straightened, Vera clasped her hand a little tighter.

'Don't leave it so long next time,' she said, brusquely.

'Another thirty years?' Cathy laughed lightly, 'no Mum, I'll be back in a day or so.'

'Make sure you do, I'll be dead soon,' said Vera curtly, but Cathy didn't miss the mischievous spark in her eyes.

'Man, I wish I could turn the clock back,' said Cathy to Andrew as they pulled out of the driveway. 'If I'd only known Vera as an adult, I think we'd have been such friends.'

'She's a character.' Andrew chuckled softly. 'Always was, you know.'

Cathy rubbed the space between her brows. 'Really? I don't remember that. Life seemed to be an endless round of uncertainty and trying to figure out which parent was the lesser of two evils. Dad was a tyrant - I mean, he really was - but Mum's unpredictability was harder to deal with in some ways. I felt I could read my father so much easier. I recall feeling drained all the time, anxious and desperate to please.' She sighed.

'And now?'

She looked at him. 'I was terrified to meet Vera again.'

'You didn't let it show.'

Cathy gave a rueful smile. 'Years of practice,' she said simply.

The mood in the car had taken a sombre turn. Seeing Vera again had shaken Cathy to the core. Her emotions were all over the place. The mother she knew had been an explosive combination of high drama, loud laughter and gut-wrenching despair. Everything was to the extreme - Vera's moods, her dazzling beauty, style and love could all vanish on the flip of a coin, leaving Cathy a confused little girl, walking on eggshells. And now, for the first time, she could see the woman behind the mask; still spirited, still pushing the boundaries and holding on to her dignity with all her might. How had this irrepressible life force become so damaged? Alcohol and abuse and children who were too frightened to love her. Vera must have been so lonely, thought Cathy and the realisation broke her heart.

TWENTY-FOUR

Cathy couldn't sleep. In the morning, she told Andrew she'd decided to go back to Honeysuckle Lodge and have a proper talk with Vera.

Sammy was due back in town and Cathy was glad to give he and Andy some space, but agreed to meet up with them later for dinner at the outdoor dining precinct near the flat. She picked up a hire car and navigated her way out of London, feeling more and more like a local.

The drive down to Kent gave Cathy time by herself to think about what she wanted to ask her mother. She had so many questions.

A new face, whose name badge said Stella, opened the front door. The office door was closed this time and Cathy assumed Monica Jackson didn't work on Sundays, and there was no sigh of Helen Peterson either. The home seemed quieter than the day before. Cathy wondered if some of the residents were out with relatives and was pleased she'd thought to pick up some flowers for Vera. She signed in, pumped a dollop of antibacterial soap into her hand and made her way to Vera's room.

She found her mother again seated in the armchair, this time with a book in her hand. It was a jolt to realise she had no idea what her mother liked to read and Cathy resolved to find out and buy her some new titles. Perhaps they could go into Tunbridge Wells together; have lunch at a cafe on The Pantiles, take a stroll through town.

'Hi Mum,' Cathy bent to give her mother a kiss, 'these are for you.' She held out the flowers, stylishly wrapped in brown paper and twine and when Vera stared but didn't take them, Cathy laid the bouquet on the side table. 'I'll find a vase in a minute,' she said and pulled up the second chair. 'How're you feeling today?'

Vera regarded her. 'Hello dear,' she said in a neutral tone and Cathy felt a twinge of panic that her mother had forgotten who she was.

'It's Cathy,' she said, feeling rather foolish.

'Yes.'

Cathy cleared her throat. 'I'm by myself today. Andrew isn't here because his partner's coming home from touring with a dance company. I haven't met Sammy yet, but we're all catching up for dinner later.'

Vera watched her closely. 'Who is Sammy?'

'Andy's partner.'

'Wife?'

'Boyfriend.'

Vera let that piece of information settle for a moment. 'I'm glad Andrew has someone,' she said eventually. 'I always worried about him being by himself so much. He had you of course when you were children but he got sent off to boarding school and then he was at university somewhere...'

'Newcastle,' said Cathy.

'Was it? Well once the twins and then you and your father left, I saw very little of Andrew or his parents so I really couldn't say where he was.'

Cathy remembered Andy's comment about Vera being a recluse in her own home and wondered who had stopped contacting who.

'Pass me my bag would you?' said Vera abruptly. A solid-looking leather handbag was sitting on top of a chest of drawers on the other side of the room.

Cathy obeyed and placed it on her mother's lap.

'Thank you.' Vera opened the bag and retrieved a small glass bottle. Cathy gaped in horror.

'What are you doing? You can't drink in here.'

Vera poured vodka into a tumbler on the table at her side. 'Of course I can. It's a free country.'

Cathy shot a quick look to the open bedroom door. 'What if one of the staff comes in?'

Her mother paused with the drink in her hand. 'Let them. It doesn't bother me.'

Cathy hesitated, half wanting to run and find Helen Peterson and half wanting Vera to do what she liked. Was there really much harm in a little nip?

Vera downed it in one, gave a satisfied sigh and set the glass back on the table.

'Much better,' she said. 'Now if I could just find my cigarettes.'

'Let's go outside,' said Cathy quickly. 'Would you show me the garden?'

Vera snorted. 'What garden? A few shrubs out the front and a bit of lawn.'

Cathy remembered the broken fountain. 'I'd like to sit round by the gate. I saw some benches there when I drove in.'

Vera didn't bother to hide her distain. 'Suit yourself,' she said, 'help me up, then.'

As they left the bedroom, Vera leaned heavily on Cathy's arm and allowed herself to be guided through the house. Stella appeared with a bundle of washing in her arms.

'Going out for a bit of fresh air? Good idea, ladies. Vera, do you need your cardigan? I'll fetch it for you.'

Vera rolled her eyes but didn't comment and she and Cathy made it to the front door.

'Let's make a bid for freedom,' said Vera in a husky undertone.

'Ha, yes,' said Cathy, 'but I think we must be Tunbridge Wells's worst escapees. We haven't even got our jackets.'

Vera chuckled.

STELLA ARRIVED BEARING a thick knitted cardigan and plaid blanket.

'Here you are,' she said cheerfully and lifted Vera's arm to feed it into the cardigan sleeve.

'I can do it,' grumbled Vera, 'stop flapping.'

Without comment, Stella proceeded to drape the blanket over her knees as well.

'Good heavens girl, it's not Arctic conditions,' muttered Vera. Cathy looked on, feeling useless, while her mother huffed and tutted throughout, and when Stella had the audacity to suggest a pair of gloves, the old lady's minimal patience evaporated altogether.

'Do fuck *off* dear,' she said mildly. Cathy gasped in horror, but Stella ignored the comment and tucked the blanket in more securely.

'There you are, nice and snug. I'll bring you ladies a cup of tea,' she said with a little grin to Cathy.

'Thank you,' said Cathy, mortified and hugely amused at the same time.

Stella hurried off and disappeared into the comfortable house behind them.

'Where is everyone today?' said Cathy. 'It's so quiet.'

'Off gallivanting on the bus.' Vera folded her hands in her lap.

Cathy recalled Helen Peterson saying Vera was always keen for an outing. 'Didn't you want to go, Mum?'

'Not today.'

'What's wrong with today?'

Vera pursed her lips.

Cathy pushed a bit harder. 'Don't you feel well?'

Vera's shoulders twitched. 'I thought you might come for another visit.' She sniffed as though she couldn't care less.

'Oh Mum.' Cathy pulled her mother in for a hug and felt Vera's tense body soften. She briefly rested her cheek on Cathy's shoulder and then pulled back.

'Alright alright, don't get emotional.'

Cathy disentangled herself and leaned against the back of the bench.

'You're a funny one,' she said affectionately.

'Huh.'

There was a pause.

'There's no ring on your finger - why haven't you got a husband?' said Vera suddenly.

'I did have one, years ago.'

'What happened to him?'

'It didn't work out, Mum.'

Vera gave an impatient click of her tongue. 'You've got to make an effort you know. Happy marriages don't just happen.'

'Were you happy with Dad?'

Vera's face closed down. 'We didn't talk about such things in those days.'

'Well it's not those days any more. I think you should talk about it if you want to.'

'What's the point? It's all in the past.'

'God, what is it with you and Auntie Dot - both of you are so keen to avoid talking about the past. I thought you lot would love to chat about the good old days.'

'What do you want to know?'

Cathy gazed at her. *Everything.*

She picked her words carefully. 'I guess I want to know when things started to go wrong. Was it this?' She tapped the side of Vera's handbag. 'The bottle?'

'Oh, that's never been a problem. Let me tell you, it helped.'

'Talk to me about Dad. Why was he such an angry man?'

Vera's eyes misted. 'Edward was marvellous. So bright. And clever,' she hit the arm of the bench for emphasis, 'a true creative. Wonderful mind. And such fun.'

Cathy listened incredulously. 'When though? When he was young?'

Vera nodded, her voice a wistful echo of her usual gruff tone. 'The sixties were incredible and we lived it all. My dear, the stories...' She tailed off.

'He was ghastly to you,' murmured Cathy, unable to believe they were talking about the same man.

'Edward? Oh he had a very stressful job you know. I probably got on his nerves.'

Cathy's disbelief hardened. 'He hit you, Mum.'

'I expect I deserved it.'

'No you didn't! And neither did the boys. And neither did I.'

Vera's mouth fell open.

'You can't deny it Mum. You might have tried to blank it out, but I haven't. Mark and Paul haven't.'

'How would you know? You don't talk to any of your family.'

'Don't turn this back onto me.' Cathy's face burned. She bit back a torrent of accusations. *Where were you when your children were crying? Where were you when we needed our mum? Why didn't you protect us, why didn't you leave him?*

There was a palpable tension now. Cathy struggled to diffuse it.

'I don't want to fight with you,' she said eventually.

Vera had turned to stone.

'I think it's time you went home,' she said coldly. 'I'm going back to my room.'

TWENTY-FIVE

The last thing Cathy felt like doing was going out for dinner with Andrew and Sammy. She already feared being the third wheel, especially as they hadn't seen one another for a good couple of weeks. She felt drained and upset after her morning with Vera and didn't want to be Deputy Downer and spoil Sammy's homecoming.

When she got back to the flat, Andrew was out and Cathy was grateful for the spare key he'd given her that morning. She texted to say she was home and then went to lie down in the cool blue bedroom.

Vera had frustrated the life out of her, but Cathy already knew she'd be heading back to Tunbridge Wells the following day. She so wanted her mother to be honest and open about their life on The Narrows. Perhaps a new day would bring the right words, so Cathy could find a way to break through Vera's defences.

She slid into a deep comforting sleep and when she awoke, it was dark. There was a message from Andrew suggesting they meet at 7.30pm. Cathy got up, had a shower and changed into fresh clothes. Already she felt better and left the flat, turning up her jacket collar against a sharp early evening wind. The balmy weather of recent days had deserted the London streets.

Andrew and Sammy were holed up at a table near the front of the mall. They sat close, their foreheads nearly touching. Cathy almost retreated and went home, not wanting to walk in and break their lovely bubble. Andrew's face was lit with a glowing aura of contentment as he smiled broadly at something Sammy was saying and even from her spot out on the pavement, Cathy could see Sammy was a stunning young man, with thick wavy black hair and slender hands. She hesitated, but then Andy glanced up and caught her eye. In that moment, Cathy loved him more than she ever had; he looked so blissfully happy and her heart swelled with gratitude that one of The Narrows children at least, had found true happiness.

Sammy was a total charmer and had Andrew and Cathy in fits of laughter with tales of life on the road. He was a born storyteller, but didn't monopolise the conversation and was as good a listener as he was raconteur. When he got up to go to the bathroom, Andrew didn't hesitate.

'What do you think?' He clasped Cathy's hand.

'I love him,' she said. 'You two are perfect together.'

'God, I'm so relieved. I really wanted you to like him.'

'He's a keeper.' Cathy gave Andy a quick kiss on the cheek, but his face suddenly clouded.

'There's quite a big age gap,' he started, but Cathy cut him off.

'So what? Be in the moment, enjoy *this*. If you try to predict the future, you'll end up living in a state of constant worry. You and Sammy are here right now and anyone can see you adore each other.'

He exhaled. 'Thank you.' And then, 'hey, how did it go with Auntie Vera today?'

'Ah,' Cathy scrunched up her nose, 'not great. We had a few terse words. Firstly I couldn't get her to talk about the past and then when she did, it was to tell me what an incredible man my father was. It's as though she has obliterated all memories of him being an asshole - no, worse - a domineering bully who we were all afraid of.'

'I'm sorry,' said Andrew sincerely, 'for all of it. And one of the really sad things is that being in such a difficult environment didn't bring you closer to your brothers.'

Cathy shrugged. 'They had each other. We've always been friendly, but to be honest I don't think they supported me any more than I supported them.'

'What about Auntie Vera - will you visit her again?'

'For sure. I can't hold a grudge forever, but I wish she'd trust me enough to be truthful. It makes me sad to think of her seeing out her days with no family around her, but then I remember why. I really don't think she did anything to shield us. America seemed like a viable option, even though it meant spending more time with my father in the early days.

Not that I had any choice in the matter. Anyway,' she said as
Sammy reappeared, weaving through crowded tables
towards them, 'in answer to your question, yes I'll be heading
down to Honeysuckle Lodge again tomorrow morning, if
only to say goodbye.'

HELEN PETERSON INTERCEPTED Cathy at the sign-in book.

'Just a heads-up,' she said gently, 'Vera isn't at her best,
today.'

Cathy put the pen down. 'She's drinking?'

'We've had a lot of tears. She was up in the night as well,
roaming around, quite distressed.'

Cathy's face tightened. 'That could be my fault. I visited
her yesterday and it didn't end very well. I have a lot of...' she
stopped as a resident appeared at the top of the corridor,
leaning into her walker as she gradually made her way
towards them.

Helen patted Cathy's arm, 'pop into the office, I'll settle
Patricia in the lounge and be right in.'

Cathy nodded, relieved. In the office, Monica Jackson was
on the phone. She smiled at Cathy and pointed to an empty
chair.

It was comforting to be around these capable women. For
most of Cathy's adult life, Vera had occupied minimal space
in her mind, but now she was here, how thankful she was
that such dedicated professionals were in her mother's life.

'Now then.' Helen bustled in and sat down heavily behind

her desk. 'Let's start again. Sorry to ambush you in the hall-way, but I didn't want you to go in unprepared. You were saying?'

Cathy lifted her head, ashamed now of her impatience with Vera.

'I don't know how much you're aware of,' she said slowly, 'but my mother's relationships with her children were badly damaged when we were kids. I look at Vera today and I see a lonely, defenceless person clinging to her rose-tinted specta-cles and refusing to admit what happened years ago. All my life, I've felt angry with both my parents and would love for one of them to acknowledge their mistakes and maybe even apologise, but I know it's never going to happen with my father and after seeing Vera yesterday, I don't think it will ever happen with her, either. She simply doesn't get it.'

Helen's eyes were warm with compassion. 'If it helps at all, I can tell you she does get it,' she said. 'There have been a few occasions during Vera's time at Honeysuckle Lodge when her bravado has crumbled. Admittedly, it's usually when she's had a drink or two, but nonetheless, the staff have heard some pretty upsetting stories.'

Cathy pushed her hair from her forehead. 'They're so good with her. Stella was wonderful yesterday and I'm sorry to say Vera actually swore at her. Nobody should come to work and be sworn at.'

Helen gave a little smile. 'We understand sometimes our residents aren't themselves. I'm sure Vera didn't mean any harm.' She paused. 'I heard you brought your mother some flowers?'

Cathy glanced up, puzzled. 'Yes. That's okay isn't it?'

'Absolutely, but I think it took her by surprise. She told Stella later, that nobody had given her flowers before.'

'Ever?' Cathy's eyebrows rose.

'Never ever, so she didn't know how to accept them.'

'Oh how sad. Poor Mum.'

Helen nodded. 'She really is suffering,' she said quietly, 'I just thought you should know.'

TWENTY-SIX

Vera was lying on her bed, crying.

Cathy pulled the chair up close and stroked her hair, stiff with lacquer.

Her mother flinched and twisted round to face her. Her blouse was ruched. She looked hot and uncomfortable and her lined face was smeared with tears, but she valiantly struggled into a sitting position.

Cathy helped her, surprised by how heavy she was; a dead weight too weary to function properly.

Silently she fetched a box of tissues and placed them on the bed, then busied herself with pouring a glass of water. Anything to avoid looking at Vera's devastation.

They sat there for a moment, the elderly lady on the brink of giving up and the tense younger woman biting back tears of her own. Day to day sounds of the nursing home wafted in through the open door.

Finally, Cathy gathered her courage.

'I'm sorry about yesterday,' she said.

Vera clamped her mouth shut.

'I didn't come here to upset you,' said Cathy gently.

There was a stifled sound and Cathy could see her mother's face fiercely working, as she fought for her composure. She gave a sharp shake of her head.

'You have nothing...' she muttered hoarsely, 'to apologise for. I'm the one who should say sorry. I failed you. You and Paul and Mark, my precious babies.'

'Mum...' started Cathy, but Vera cut across her.

'I was weak. *Weak.* And I let that man destroy me.' She juddered in pain. 'I'm so sorry, Cathy.'

Cathy's heart unlocked and all the hurts and sorrows of Vera's past poured in. 'Please don't cry. What could you do? You were trapped there - three children, no money, nowhere to go...I'm not angry with you, I only want to know about my life.'

'Yes,' said Vera as she blotted her swollen eyes, her voice now steadier. 'You deserve to know.'

'I LOVED EDWARD, ONCE,' said Vera dreamily. 'When we were young, he was the most dazzling man. We had fun together, he made me laugh. In the early days, I felt like a queen.'

Cathy regarded her. 'What went wrong?'

Vera switched back in, her soft memories solidifying into something hard. 'I saw changes when the twins were born.

Despite his assurances to the contrary, I don't think he saw me as desirable any more. A lumpy tummy; leaky breasts.' She sighed. 'And I tried, believe me, I really tried. I made sure I looked good for him, but in order for that to happen, I had to be so strict with myself. Eventually, I discovered the booze and ciggies diet and that worked a treat.'

'How awful. You should never have to change yourself to please somebody else.'

Vera held up her hand. 'It was my job to look the part.'

Cathy stiffened, but held back from commenting.

'It wasn't all bad though,' continued Vera, 'I had a decent allowance - I mean, he was generous, so I soon added shopping to my list of addictions.' She gave a bitter half-laugh. 'He had a roving eye, you know.'

'The babysitter?'

'Amongst others. I had to up my game - some of those girls were very young.'

Cathy shuddered. 'He's repulsive,' she muttered.

'Times were different then,' said Vera.

It was heartbreaking to see her mother desperately hanging on to some sort of justification for Edward's behaviours, but Cathy couldn't let it go. She leaned closer. 'What about the abuse though? You can't excuse him for that. *Don't* say you deserved to be hit; I won't accept it.'

Vera's eyes clouded. 'It was better for him to hit me, than any of my children.'

'That's ridiculous! And besides, he *did* hit us. He was an utter monster. I feel like you haven't grasped the extent of it all. Do you know what went on, or were you too blind drunk to notice? I mean, seriously.' Cathy pulled up. She took a moment to gather herself.

'I'm sorry,' whispered Vera.

Cathy could hardly look at her. Her vulnerability was shocking. The bloodshot eyes were already filling again.

'Why did you come back?' said Vera wearily. 'This...hashing over what happened years ago isn't going to change anything. Why did you come back now?'

'I told you, Mum. Uncle Eric died.' Cathy hesitated. 'And actually, he left me some money in his will. I had an email...letter...from his solicitor.'

'I know what an email is,' countered Vera. She paused. 'How much money?'

'A lot. A million pounds.'

Vera's pallor flushed dark red. 'Good heavens.'

'Uncle Eric left Andrew a substantial amount too. And Dot of course.'

Vera nodded and then changed tack.

'Have you been in touch with Andrew over the years?'

'A little. Online a bit, you know, here and there, but massive chunks of our lives were never covered. We only knew very basic things, like where we lived. It's been lovely to reconnect with him again.'

'Well of course,' Vera smoothed an invisible crease in her skirt, 'you two were always such pals.'

Cathy couldn't stop herself. 'But Mum, I needed *you* to be my pal. I needed you. Why did I end up with my father? I feel like you could have stopped him from taking me to

America. I was only sixteen, still a girl. Where was my mother in all of this?'

Vera bit back hard. 'He had custody!' She furiously swiped her hand across her eyes. 'I had nothing to offer you, not a single thing.'

'Except your love! That would have been enough - more than enough. Why couldn't you love me, Mum?'

'I did love you. I *do* love you, it was Edward who couldn't...' she broke off, weeping.

'What? What couldn't he do?'

Vera put both hands over her face. Cathy fought the temptation to knock them away.

'Speak to me!' she commanded. 'What couldn't Edward do?'

Vera gulped through her fingers, her head bowed.

'He wanted to separate us, to cause me the most hurt but he couldn't accept you, Cathy. He just couldn't.'

'Why not? Cathy's heart hammered wildly. 'Tell me!'

'He's not your father!'

There was a stunned silence. Cathy's brain froze. She took her mother by the shoulders and forced her to meet her eyes.

'What did you say?' Her voice was oddly flat. She felt detached.

Vera pulled her crimson swollen face away, sobs still rattling through her chest.

'Edward is not your father. Eric was.'

Cathy dropped her hands like hot coals. She narrowed her eyes. 'How much have you had to drink?' she hissed.

Vera vehemently shook her head. 'It's not the booze talking. I'm your mother and Eric was your father.'

Cathy leapt to her feet and moved to the farthest corner of the room. Cold and sick, her whole world was spinning.

'I'm sorry, wavered Vera, 'so sorry, Cathy.'

Cathy leaned against the chest of drawers with her arms clamped across her chest. She tried to unravel the white noise in her head.

'So you, what? Had an affair with...with Uncle Eric? Why? To get back at Edward?' There was a crash of pieces cascading into place. 'And that's why Karen divorced him?' One hand covered her mouth. 'Does Andrew know?'

Vera cried and rocked, sobbing hoarsely as she struggled to speak.

'I'm sorry, I'm sorry...'

Cathy pushed herself off the chest of drawers and strode out of the room.

TWENTY-SEVEN

Helen and Monica were at their desks when Cathy gave two sharp raps on the office door and barged in.

'Goodness...' Startled, Helen got to her feet. 'What's wrong? Is Vera alright?'

'I don't know. Helen, I really need to speak to you.'

'Of course.' She eased out from behind her desk. 'Sit, sit...'

'Can we go outside?'

Helen glanced at Monica. 'Would you mind...?' She took Cathy's arm. 'What happened? Did Vera fall?'

'No,' said Cathy as Monica hurried from the room, 'she's upset though.'

'Come with me.' Helen guided her out into the hallway and through the front door.

Cathy breathed in a mouthful of crisp fresh air. Goosebumps stood out on her arms. They went to the benches by the gate.

'My mother is rambling,' said Cathy, running an agitated hand through her hair. 'She claims my father isn't who I thought he was. It's bizarre and frankly it scared me. I don't know if she's making it up or if it's real, or what.'

Helen listened, her hands resting in her lap. 'As we know, Vera is in the early stages of dementia so I wouldn't advise blindly accepting everything she says. I think the best thing is for you to have a talk with our Director of Pastoral Care, Thomas. I happen to know he's had a number of conversations with Vera and while he's not going to betray a confidence, if he can help you, he will. He's due in at 11.00 this morning so why don't you go to the chapel and meet him there? I'll let him know you're coming.'

'I don't know...' muttered Cathy, 'what is he? Some sort of clergyman? I can't see my mother confiding in a man of the cloth, somehow.' She faced Helen squarely. 'What has Vera told you?'

'Nothing like this,' replied Helen, 'and I think you should consider talking to Thomas. He's a lovely person - it might help.'

Cathy fidgeted. 'Okay fine,' she said reluctantly, 'but I ought to go back to Vera's room first. She was pretty distressed.'

'Monica went to check on her, so don't worry. Take a break, regroup and when you feel ready, go back to Vera.' She looked at her watch. 'Thomas will be here in half an hour anyway.'

'Thank you.' Cathy fished her phone from her pocket. 'I'll stay out here for a bit. I need to call my cousin.'

Two men were talking in the chapel doorway when Cathy turned up. The younger man - Thomas she assumed - smiled at her as she slipped past and went to sit down. The chapel was really only a room at the back of the house, but it was cool and the atmosphere one of quiet reflection. Just being in there made Cathy feel better.

The murmured conversation in the doorway ended and the resident, a straight-backed man with groomed silver hair, moved back into the main part of the house and disappeared.

The younger man walked over the Cathy and extended his hand.

'Hi, Thomas Bagshaw.'

She stood up. 'Cathy Douglas. Hello, I'm Vera Douglas's daughter.'

'Ah yes, I heard you were over from America. Nice to meet you.' Thomas gestured for her to resume her seat, and sat down too. 'What part of the States are you from?'

'California. The Napa Valley.'

'Not too nippy for you here I hope?'

'No, I was born not too far from Tunbridge Wells actually, so I know what to expect.'

There was a pause.

'How can I help?'

Cathy studied Thomas's kind, open face. He looked about her own age, she thought.

'Are you a pastor, or...?'

'No no, we are a non-denominational chapel.'

'I understand, but what religion are you?'

He smiled at her forthright manner. 'I'm in the market.'

Cathy nodded. 'Very diplomatic.'

'I'm here for whatever our residents need, from a spiritual point of view.'

'You must be a good listener.'

'I hope so.'

Cathy cleared her throat. 'Okay, so you know my mother?'

'I do indeed.'

'Ha. What does that mean?'

Thomas grinned. 'Not a thing.'

Cathy relaxed into a smile, too. 'She can be a handful, I know.'

'Your mother is a beautiful lady. Inquisitiveness can be a rare commodity in a place like Honeysuckle Lodge.'

'Oh God, I bet she bombards you with questions about death and whether she's going to hell.'

He shrugged slightly. 'She has a curious mind. Nothing wrong with that.'

Cathy hesitated. 'She's quite unwell, I don't know if you're aware.'

Thomas's expression gave nothing away.

'She's an alcoholic.'

He nodded.

'And has dementia. Early stages, but still.'

'Mmm.'

'Thomas, look Vera is saying some really weird things. This morning she told me my father isn't actually my father at all. The thing is, I don't know whether or not to believe her.'

'Do you want to believe her?'

The question caught Cathy off guard. 'I don't know.'

'Is the man in question still alive?'

Cathy shook her head. 'He died recently and left me a legacy.'

'Did it surprise you?'

'It did and it didn't. He was my uncle and I'd always been close to him and to his son, my cousin Andrew. We were best friends until my father - or who I've always *thought* was my father - divorced my mother, got custody of me and took me to America.'

'How old were you when that happened?'

'Sixteen.'

Thomas didn't comment.

'My problem,' said Cathy slowly, 'is this. I don't know if Vera is deliberately lying, or whether she's muddled because of her condition, or confused because she's drunk.'

'Perhaps she's being truthful.'

'Yes,' admitted Cathy. 'Perhaps she is.'

There was a small silence.

'Has she ever spoken to you about the past?' said Cathy finally.

'Many times. She has happy memories of being young.'

'In the sixties?' Cathy shook her head. 'She's even tried to convince *me* it was a wonderful life, when I remember clearly what it was like. It was appalling. Her husband abused her and us kids and she hit the bottle pretty hard. I used to long to get away from the house and go to live with my uncle, aunt and cousin up the road. I felt safe there, I felt wanted and it's messing with my head to think perhaps I *should* have been there all along.'

'Is there anybody who could verify what Vera is saying?' said Thomas gently. 'A family member...friend...?'

'I tried to call my cousin earlier, but it rang out. I'm staying with him though so I'll see him later.'

'And your aunt - is she still alive?'

'Yes, but I don't know, I don't want to freak her out if it's all a load of rubbish.'

'No.'

'Okay,' said Cathy after a moment or two, 'well thank you for your time, Thomas. It helped to talk it through.'

'You're welcome. It was very nice to meet you.'

Cathy stood and glanced around. 'I like your chapel.'

Thomas dipped his head. 'Thank you.'

She smiled as they shook hands. 'No doubt I'll see you again before I go home,' she said.

'Call in any time,' he said kindly, 'the chapel is always open.'

TWENTY-EIGHT

Cathy made her way back to Vera's room. The chat with Thomas had gone some way to clearing her mind, but still she felt rattled and hurt. When she peeped into the room though, Vera was asleep. Cathy stepped away and ducked into the office to say she was leaving.

'I'll be back tomorrow,' she said and Helen, composed as ever, simply nodded.

While she had every intention of driving straight back to London, Cathy found herself veering towards The Narrows. The pull to get answers was strong enough for her to risk unsettling Dot, bearing in mind her aunt may not be able to confirm or deny anything. Cathy knew she was putting Dot in a difficult situation and rehearsed what she might say.

Her opening lines were dashed however, when Dot opened the door. In all the confusing narrative knocking through her head, Cathy had let slip the fact that Dot's husband had died. She looked older than the previous week. More frail. Less energised.

'Hi Auntie,' said Cathy and was suddenly transported back to her ten-year-old self, rapping on their front door, escaping the turmoil at home. 'I wanted to come and see you.'

Dot's face broke into a tired smile. 'Of course, Cathy. Come in.' She stood aside for her niece to cross the threshold.

They went into the kitchen and Dot switched on the kettle.

'Take a seat, dear.'

'I'm sorry to barge in like this, but I really need to talk to you,' said Cathy, pulling out a kitchen chair.

Dot retrieved a couple of teabags and went to the fridge for milk.

Cathy pressed on. 'I've been to visit Mum this morning and the staff said she'd been drinking and upset during the night. Things got a bit heated and she said some strange things and I don't know what to believe. Maybe you'll be able to help me.'

Dot came to sit down. 'I don't know if I can shed any light on anything your mother is saying, Cathy. I haven't seen Vera for years.'

'This is about the past,' said Cathy, watching Dot's face, 'and in particular, my childhood. Vera told me Edward isn't actually my dad.' She raised her shoulders. 'Is it true?'

Dot frowned. 'Vera said that?'

Cathy moistened her lips. 'Is it true, Auntie?'

Dot gave a sorrowful shake of her head. 'Vera must be getting muddled, to tell you such a thing.'

'Drunk, you mean?'

'I didn't say that, Cathy.'

'It's a possibility though. Either it was alcohol, or the dementia is worse, or she's speaking the truth.'

'What did the staff say?'

'They don't know either.'

'You asked them?'

'Yes,' said Cathy, surprised at Dot's rather spiky question. 'I even had a chat with the Pastoral Care Director.'

Her aunt studied her. 'Well I'm sure it has nothing to do with me,' she said with finality and got up to make the tea.

It was difficult to know how to broach the subject of Eric and Vera's supposed affair, but Cathy burned to know if they were really her true parents. She started cautiously.

'I never knew why Eric and Karen divorced,' she said as casually as possible.

'Deep creases appeared on Dot's brow. 'Why is that relevant?'

Cathy spread her hands. 'I'm trying to unravel a lot of threads and not getting very far. I'm sorry Auntie, I didn't mean to cause offence.'

'I'm not offended,' said Dot, 'merely curious. But in answer to your question, all I know about Karen is she made off and left poor Eric alone. It shocked me actually, as I always thought Karen was a sweet girl. Eric was bereft.'

Cathy took it in. 'Where did she go?'

'I have no idea. When Eric and I got together, she had long gone. Your mother might be able to help you with that, she and Karen were best friends years ago.'

'Did you know Edward was abusive?' asked Cathy abruptly.

Dot visibly blanched.

'To be honest, I think you must have known,' continued Cathy, 'didn't you wonder why I was always round here?'

'You and Andrew were the best of friends.'

'Come on Auntie, Andy told me himself it was pretty obvious what was going on. It's beyond belief to think nobody did anything to help.'

Dot folded her arms. 'Well don't look at me, dear. I worked for Edward. I wasn't about to go round accusing him of something like that.'

'No,' said Cathy, frowning slightly, 'when Andrew was born you were married to Eric. So when Andy and me used to play together as kids, Edward wouldn't have been your boss then.'

'Why are you interrogating me about all this? All I can tell you is Eric didn't do anything wrong, Andrew didn't do anything wrong and I certainly didn't. Any misery and unhappiness that took place was in your home, not mine.'

It was Cathy's turn to flinch.

'Vera didn't confide in me,' added Dot indignantly. 'She didn't even like me.'

'Why? Because Karen had gone? Were you a bit keen to jump into her shoes?'

'Cathy!' Dot's expression darkened. 'I've got nothing to tell you,' she said flatly. 'Talk to your parents.'

Cathy slumped.

Her aunt put a cup of tea in front of her.

'Sugar?'

'No thank you.'

Dot settled down and stirred her tea, clearly done with the conversation.

It was hopeless.

TWENTY-NINE

Cathy drove back to London feeling flat. The snow globe of her life had been picked up and shaken, with all the snowflakes landing in places which made no sense. Could Eric really be her father? She thought about the million pounds. She thought about Dot. And Andrew. She was dying to talk to him.

She dropped the car back and made for Andrew's place, on automatic. She was getting used to the buzzing streets, sudden rainfall, kaleidoscope of faces, screeching brakes. The Napa Valley seemed a lifetime away.

Andy was home, at one with the couch, on the phone. Cathy raised her hand to say hello as she tiptoed to the bedroom.

'Hiya, you alright?' He had finished the call and was right outside the door.

'Hey, yes - be out in a minute.'

'Fancy a drink?'

'It's a bit early, but I'd love one.'

'Slippery slope!'

Cathy caught the lightness in his voice and felt a sudden affinity with Vera. Is this how her unhealthy relationship with booze had started? Just a bit of fun, a drink to get loosened up?

She came out of the room and sank onto the sofa.

'What a fucking morning.'

Andy took a step backwards. 'Wow - that bad?'

'Today I've talked to a nurse, an alcoholic, a spiritual advisor and a widow.'

'Is this the start of some terrible joke?'

'No joke, Cuz. Vera is spouting some pretty strange shit and I've gotta tell you, I'm struggling to believe a word of it, but when I went to see Dot...'

'You visited Mum?'

'I needed clarification. I have so many questions.'

'About what?' Andrew's eyes were dark with concern.

Cathy gazed at him. She pressed her knuckle briefly to her lips. 'Andy, what do you remember about our childhoods?'

'You're gonna have to expand. What, in particular are you talking about?'

She couldn't find the words. The silence stretched out.

Andy put his drink down. 'Your father?'

Cathy gulped. 'Yes.'

'Well I know I didn't like him. I know he was very strict and you didn't like him either. I know you got smacked a lot. I know there was bad blood between your parents and my parents, which I always thought was a work thing.' He opened his hands, 'what are you really asking?'

'Vera claims...' Cathy stopped. How to say this?

'Vera told me this morning that Edward isn't my biological father.' She breathed out.

Andrew's face was rigid. 'Seriously? Not your dad? Well who is, then?'

Cathy's voice dried up. The words came out in a feeble croak. 'Andy, we have to remember Vera is sick. We can't really be sure of anything she says.'

'Okay, but it's a pretty big fact to get wrong, don't you think?' His head tilted slightly, 'this is huge for you. Jesus.' He took her hot hands. 'Who is your father if it's not Edward?'

Cathy's eyes were huge. She must not cry.

'Andy, she said it was Eric.'

It took a moment to register. Andrew withdrew his hands and stood up. Cathy watched him with a thumping heart.

'Uh...' He stopped. 'My father was also your father?'

She nodded, waves of panic flooding through her as she took deep breath after deep breath.

Andy's hand went to his mouth. *'Fuck.'*

Cathy sat on the very edge of her seat, gripping her arms, biting her lip.

'How?' said Andy, 'I mean, why? Holy shit, is this the reason Karen left Eric?' Colour rushed into his cheeks. 'Dad and *Vera*?' He paced the small room, holding his head. 'Does Mum know?'

'She says she doesn't know anything.'

'You *asked* her?'

'No, no not exactly. I was fishing, trying to find out if she could verify what Vera told me.'

Andy stopped moving. 'And?'

'Like I said, Dot denies knowing anything. She said Karen was off the scene when she and Eric got together.'

'You didn't tell her what Vera said, did you?'

'No, of course not.'

He looked at her across the coffee table. 'Are you alright?'

'Not really, but if it's true a lot of things make sense.'

'The divorce?'

'Yes, for one.'

Andrew paused. 'And if this *is* true, you know what it means, don't you?'

'What?'

'We're not cousins, Cuz. We're brother and sister.'

Everything stopped. Andrew and Cathy stared at each other.

'Oh my God,' whispered Cathy eventually, 'you're right.' Her vision blurred.

Andy sat down next to her. 'All this time, all those years...'

She took his hand. '*If* it's true.'

'I hated being an only child. If I'd only known I had a sister...'

'Technically half sister I guess,' said Cathy quietly.

'I'll take that.'

Her nose tingled. 'Me too.'

Andrew's face crumpled. 'Why didn't anyone tell us?'

Cathy cleared her throat. 'I know I keep saying it, but Andy we can't be certain it's true.'

'It is true,' he said firmly. 'We've had that bond, all our lives. More than friends, more than cousins, despite the years of separation.' He brushed his hand across his eyes.

Cathy got up to fetch a roll of paper towels from the kitchen drawer, and tore off a couple of sheets.

Andrew blew his nose. 'How are we ever going to get to the bottom of it all? Do you think my dad and your mum really did have an affair?'

'Seems like it.'

'It's so unlike my father though,' said Andy thoughtfully. 'He came over as such a moral kind of man. Pious, almost. Why the hell did he sleep with his twin's wife? It beggars belief. And Vera, too - I mean it's shocking to think she could do that to her husband. And weren't she and Karen supposed to be the best of friends?'

Cathy shrugged. 'Don't ask me, I'm just the end product.'

Andrew gave a soft gasp. 'Cathy, I'm so sorry. I haven't even asked you how you're feeling. I'm guessing shocked doesn't really cover it.'

'Actually, I feel numb,' said Cathy. 'I'm waiting for the real pain to start, like when you stub your toe and you know it's going to hurt like hell in a second. And the pain hits and it's agony and you swear and rub your toe and cry.'

Andy's mouth twitched slightly. 'It's like stubbing your toe?'

'Okay, tiny understatement. The principle's the same though.' Cathy blew air through her slightly parted lips. 'This is nuts. All of it.'

'What do you want to do?'

'I want to find out if it's true. This could all be bullshit - I'm only going on what Vera said and what Dot *didn't* say.'

Andrew rubbed his temple. 'What about Mark and Paul? They might know something.'

Cathy considered this. 'Well I was born in 1966 when they would have been six, turning seven. I doubt they'd be aware of what the adults were doing.'

'Okay then, you'll have to ask Edward.'

Cathy gave a derisory snort. 'Not if I can help it. I want nothing to do with him.'

'Yeah, but he might be the only one to give us some answers - he was there after all. Vera's unreliable God bless her, Mum denies knowing anything and Eric is dead. So...'

'So there's only one other person I could ask.' Cathy put her shoulders back and faced him. 'Somewhere, somehow I've got to find my Auntie Karen.'

THIRTY

Next morning, Cathy called ahead before showing up at Honeysuckle Lodge; she didn't think she could deal with Vera if she was under the influence again. Her plan was to take her mother into Tunbridge Wells for lunch. Perhaps a change of scenery would help smooth out the choppy waves of their relationship a little and they'd have a chance to communicate with one another calmly.

When Cathy arrived, Vera was up, dressed and waiting in the lounge. Her hair, clothes and make-up were all immaculate and Cathy caught a glimpse of the glamorous woman she remembered. Nobody could beat that classic profile, she thought. A true beauty.

Vera was quiet this morning and Cathy felt the strain of keeping up a breezy banter, careful to avoid incendiary subjects like affairs, unwanted children and vodka. She thought about the book Vera had been reading and wished she'd taken notice of the title.

'Do you belong to the library?' asked Cathy, as she parked the car near the centre of town. The question seemed safe as houses.

'No.' Vera clambered out of the car and waited primly while Cathy gathered her belongings from the back seat. Her heart sank a little. If Vera was going to sulk all day, it would be hard going.

'But we have a nice little collection of books at Honeysuckle Lodge.'

'Great!' Cathy gave her mother a smile and took her arm. 'Let's find a bookstore and get you something new. What's your favourite book?' She racked her brains to remember the bookshelves in the lounge on The Narrows. 'Peyton Place?'

Vera sniffed. 'I prefer Valley of the Dolls, but I don't mind a bit of small-town scandal.'

'Murder mysteries? Agatha Christie?'

'Rosemary's Baby is more my thing.'

'Oh God, spawn of the devil. I hope you're not thinking of me.'

'You?' Vera kept her chin up, but Cathy didn't miss the clouds in her eyes. 'You were an angel. And you still are.'

Cathy's throat tightened. 'Thank you Mum, that's a lovely thing to say.'

Vera looked away. 'Are we getting lunch soon? I'm ravenous.'

They spent a companionable half hour in a quaint little bookshop crammed with toppling shelves. Vera dove in, picking and discarding titles and it warmed Cathy's heart to see her mother so engaged. It was great to get her out of her room where booze, cigarettes and the television seemed to be her only distractions. She had forgotten she was hungry, too.

Cathy peered over her shoulder. 'Ooh Ruth Rendell. Good choice. Come on, let me treat you.'

They left the bookshop and continued on to The Pantiles where they found a table outside, lit by watery sunshine. The Vera of years gone by was out in force, confidently studying the menu and neatly crossing her still elegant legs at the ankles. Cathy was proud of her - she understood the effort her mother was making.

They chose the same things for lunch: Frittata, salad and sparkling water. It was a relief to see Vera drinking something healthy - she was lovely company when she was sober.

It was tempting to keep the harmonious day going, with no reference to anything delicate, but Cathy had to know. Surely Vera would expect her to have questions after the bombshell of the day before. She opened the conversation tentatively, not wanting to push Vera into a defensive position too soon.

'I'm sorry I ran out on you yesterday,' she said. 'Silly of me. It was the shock of what you were saying - I panicked.'

Vera put down her knife and fork and they clinked softly on the fine white china plate. She dabbed her lips with her napkin, but didn't speak.

'When I came back you'd fallen asleep,' added Cathy.

Vera gazed at her.

'Is what you told me true?' whispered Cathy.

A nod.

Something constricted in Cathy's chest. 'Okay. It's okay Mum, I'm not mad with you but I really need to know the truth.' She cast about for the right words. 'Eric really was my father?'

'Yes.' Vera's eyes were wary.

'I'm not judging you,' said Cathy quickly. 'Please understand, I only wanted to know.'

'And now you do.'

Cathy sipped her water. 'I went to see Dot yesterday.' She risked a glance at her mother's face.

Vera's eyebrows twitched. 'What for?'

'I...'

'She's a sly one,' added Vera, warming to her theme, 'conniving, scheming little sneak. She worked for Eric and Edward - a right Miss Moneypenny, their Gal Friday, the backbone of the office. Pah!' Vera snatched up her glass. 'She chipped away at poor Eric for *years*. Long before Karen left. I never liked her; never trusted her eyes.'

'Her eyes?'

'Close together,' muttered Vera, 'far too close together. She was a mousey little thing, but determined - oh yes, she was out to get her man, I'll tell you that much.'

'Hold on.' Cathy held up her hand. 'You can't criticise her for that - Dot married Eric *after* Karen had gone.'

'And we never got an invite to the wedding, either.' Vera glared mutinously into her sparkling water.

'So,' said Cathy, struggling to keep her mother reined in, 'where did Karen go?'

Vera swiveled in her seat. 'Is there a waitress somewhere? Get me a proper drink will you?'

'Mum?'

'What?' Vera feverishly scanned the cafe.

'What about Karen?' Cathy was determined not to back down.

'What about her? Good God, what does one have to do to get served around here?'

'Where did she go? Where did Karen go when she left Eric?'

Vera waved an imperious hand. 'Away, somewhere. Who knows?'

'God*damn* it! You were friends with Karen and then you slept with her husband - you're responsible for everything that happened to me. Tell me where she is!'

'Why?' Vera zeroed in on Cathy's face. The intensity of her icy glare was disconcerting.

'I'd like to talk to her, she was married to my father and she must know things. I'm getting nowhere with you or Dot.'

'Oh, Dot,' scoffed Vera, ready to launch into another tirade against the former secretary.

'Where did Karen go?' interrupted Cathy.

Vera gave her a long, hard look. 'The West Country.'

Cathy gasped. 'Did she? You mean Devon? Cornwall...?'

'Down that way somewhere,' said Vera airily, 'but I'm talking years and years ago. She's probably dead by now.'

Cathy exhaled. 'Thank you.' She was exhausted. Prising open the oyster shell of her past was excruciating, but bit-by-bit she was filling in the blanks. Whether there would be a pearl at the end of it all remained to be seen.

'Cathy,' said Vera reaching for her, her eyes wide with sincerity, 'I really need a drink. Just a small glass of wine will do. Anything.' It was a pathetic, heartbreaking plea.

Cathy sighed heavily.

'Please darling.'

'Okay, fine. We'll find a pub.'

'Wonderful.' Vera pushed back her chair.

'First though, let me see to the bill.' Cathy went inside to pay and left her mother standing by the table straightening her skirt and patting her hair. Vera might be hard, hard work but Cathy could not resist her.

THIRTY-ONE

'The Woodcutters Arms is nice,' remarked Vera as they drove out of Tunbridge Wells. Cathy recalled seeing the olde worlde pub set back from the main road and was glad it was on the way back to Honeysuckle Lodge. A quick drink to settle her mother and then safely home for tea and cake before it got dark.

Only two other vehicles occupied the pub car park, which fronted a sweep of lawn littered with picnic tables. The beer garden was probably a popular haunt at weekends and lazy summer evenings. Today however, the pale sunshine was already disappearing and Cathy was glad to steer her mother inside.

The heavy front door opened with a sigh against a brightly hued tartan carpet, which drew a sniff of distain from Vera.

'That's new,' she said huffily and continued on to the bar

where two old timers on high stools were poring over the Racing Gazette.

The Woodcutters Arms was a study in rustic low-ceiling charm, complete with wooden beams, fireplaces and a stash of colourful Toby jugs, lined up on a shelf. The place had an unmistakable whiff of the past about it. Only a sawdust floor was missing.

A rotund, balding man in a check shirt and pullover was polishing wine glasses.

'Afternoon ladies, what can I get you?'

'I'll have a gin and tonic,' said Vera, 'make it a double and hold the ice.' She made for a high-backed wooden settle against the window.

Cathy and the bartender watched her go.

'And I'll have an orange juice please.' Cathy took out her credit card.

The man leaned over the bar. 'Want a shot of something in that?' he said with a grin.

She smiled too. 'Don't tempt me.'

Vera was rummaging about in her handbag when Cathy carried the drinks over.

'Nope,' said Cathy sternly, 'no smoking.'

Vera stopped, a cigarette lighter already in her hand.

'Well that's antisocial,' she declared crossly.

'Sure is,' replied Cathy and pulled out a chair facing her. 'Cheers.'

'Yes, cheers.' Vera took a long drink and smacked her lips together appreciatively. 'That's better.'

'Is this your local?' asked Cathy, only half-joking.

Vera gave her shrewd look. 'It used to be. I don't get out so much these days.'

In moments like this it was easy to forget Vera had dementia. Confident and articulate, she could have been ten years younger. The day out seemed to have done her a power of good and Cathy felt the time was right to get some answers.

'I'm going to look for Karen. I'd really love to sit down and have a talk with her.'

Vera reached for her gin and tonic and took another sip. 'Don't expect too much,' she said, 'Karen might be as batty as me. Or dead.'

'Yeah you keep saying that, but I'm going to try anyway.'

Vera shrugged.

'I can't help feeling,' said Cathy cautiously, 'you aren't on board with me finding her at all. What if Karen is alive and well? What if I could bring her to see you one day? You'd like that, wouldn't you?'

'Dear God,' muttered Vera, 'here we go.'

'Here we go with what? For goodness sake Mum, what's the problem? Look I'm a grown-ass fifty three year old woman. I can handle whatever it is you're not telling me, because I *know* there's more. Wouldn't you rather tell me yourself, than Karen or even Edward? Because I will ask him if I don't get any joy from you and believe me, it's the last thing I want to do. If I never see that man again it'll be too soon, but something's off and I'm dammed if I'm going to get to fifty four without finding out. So come on, spill the beans.' She swiped up her glass, frowning.

'I think I'll have another one of these,' said Vera, pointing at the gin.

'No. Not until you talk to me.'

Vera gave an exaggerated sigh. 'Fine.'

'Thank you.' Cathy collected herself. 'Did you really have an affair with Eric?'

'No.'

'What? No affair?'

'That's right.'

'Well then,' said Cathy slowly, 'what was it, a one-night stand?'

'It was more than once.' Vera put down her glass and picked it up again. 'Look it was all planned. Karen was there and everything.'

Cathy clapped one hand over her mouth. 'Jesus. The Swinging Sixties alright.'

Vera shook her head. 'The thing was, Karen couldn't conceive. She desperately wanted a child but she just couldn't have one.'

Cathy's red face drained. 'Like me. I couldn't have babies either.' She swallowed hard. 'Am I adopted?'

'No, you're mine I promise you. Mine and Eric's.'

'Did you...' Cathy's stopped. 'Did you want me?'

Vera's head dropped. 'Karen wanted you. That's why I agreed to go through with the plan.'

'What plan?'

'Lawrence Hasting and his wife Barbara came over from America and our boys got the advertising account for their cigarette company.'

'Hasting Cigarettes? I know them - I was married to their son.' The room turned liquid around her, she felt drunk on orange juice and shock. 'They helped me and Dad - Edward - get set up in New York. Did they know I wasn't his kid?'

Vera's eyes turned foggy and unfocussed. She pulled at the cuff of her blouse. 'I don't understand anything any more.'

'Mum, no! Stay with me.' Vera could not flake now. 'Try to remember. Please, this is so important.' Cathy desperately pulled her back from the brink. 'What did the Hasting people have to do with me?'

Vera gazed blankly around the room. 'I'll have another drink now...'

Cathy clamped down on her lip. The rank taste of blood ran over her tongue. 'Don't bail on me yet. Barb and Larry Hasting. What did they do?'

'I want a drink.'

'Yes okay - but listen, what about Karen? You said she lives in the West Country. Did she get remarried?'

'No babies,' said Vera, trying to catch the bartender's eye. 'She was childless. But clever...sharp as a tack.'

Cathy snapped her fingers. 'Mum! Why did Karen go there? Was it a job, a man?'

Vera lowered her arm and stared fuzzily at her daughter's face. 'Huh. She was done with men, and who could blame her? She was so much stronger than me. I couldn't leave, you see. I had you and your brothers, so where could I go? Karen, now she had flair. She loved art and design...such a pretty girl...'

Cathy craned to listen as Vera's voice wavered and slowed. 'Mum?' she said anxiously.

'Let's have a little drink. G & T would be nice.'

There was no point pressing her further. Vera had nothing left to give.

THIRTY-TWO

Cathy delivered Vera safely back to Honeysuckle Lodge, had a quick word with the staff on duty and left her mother tucking into a hearty dinner. She could hardly wait to get back to Andy's to start her search for Karen. With all her years in marketing, Cathy knew her way round social media and understood its reach.

Andrew and Sammy were in the flat when Cathy pounded up the stairs and burst in. Sammy jumped up and ran to meet her.

'I heard the news, sister-in-law!' He clapped his hands and smacked a kiss on her cheek. Beaming, Andy rose from his chair and joined in for a group hug. Cathy had never felt so loved and connected.

'Guys, I'm on a mission. Vera finally gave up some secrets - Karen went to the West Country when she and Eric broke up. I'm gonna dig around a bit online and see what I can find.'

'Oh love,' said Sammy, 'that's a long shot.'

'Yeah,' added Andrew, 'it would have been before I was even born.'

'A *long* time ago.' Sammy prodded Andy's ribs, 'right old-timer?'

'Can I borrow your laptop?' interrupted Cathy, retrieving it from the bookshelf.

'Sleuthing!' cried Sammy joyously and scurried to sit next to her.

'I'll make a cuppa tea then shall I?' Andrew good-naturedly made for the kitchen.

'Alrighty.' Cathy opened the Internet browser and typed in the only name she had for her aunt. Karen Douglas.

'Wouldn't Karen be in her eighties by now?' Andrew abandoned the kettle and joined the others on the couch.

'Uh - yeah, late seventies early eighties I guess,' said Cathy busily scrolling past several Karen Douglasses who appeared to be in a much younger age group.

'I don't know if someone that old would be on Facebook...' Andy craned to see.

'Hmmm.' Cathy's hands stilled on the keys. 'Let me think. She may have another surname now. Vera made it pretty clear Karen had sworn off men but there could be plenty of reasons why she abandoned the Douglas name.'

'What's her maiden name?'

'Search me. But...' said Cathy, brightening up, 'Vera made a point of saying Karen was arty - she sounds creative.'

'Back in the 1960s maybe,' said Andrew doubtfully. 'I can't see how that would necessarily apply to a little old lady of eighty three though.'

'Your mother would probably know,' muttered Cathy, 'but I'm not asking her again.'

'Give me that.' Sammy expertly scrolled through page after page. 'For God's sake,' he said crossly after a couple of minutes, 'there's ten million people on here all called Karen something.' He flumped back in disgust.

Cathy slid the laptop back onto her knees. 'Let's look for all the Karen Douglasses in Cornwall and Devon.'

'What about Dorset, or Somerset?'

'Yep.'

'And Gloucestershire.' Andrew was back.

Then Sammy again. 'And Herefordshire. And Wiltshire.'

Cathy drew in a deep breath. 'Look I'm gonna search south-west England in general and see what comes up.'

'We should check Twitter and LinkedIn,' said Andy pulling out his phone.

'Bags doing Twitter,' cried Sammy, now full re-engaged.

Cathy blocked them out and kept checking and re-checking Facebook. 'Karen Douglas, K Douglas,' she mumbled. 'Nope nope nope. This is hopeless. Anything, boys?'

Andy wrinkled his nose. 'Not yet. Sammy?'

'Nah.'

'It's unlikely we'll find her,' said Andrew eventually. 'With her age and everything - I mean how many octogenarians do you know on social media?'

'Me personally?' Sammy looked up in surprise. 'None.'

'Well then.'

Cathy distractedly scratched her forehead. 'Goddammit!' she cried, 'I haven't tried Google.'

Sammy gasped. 'Okay everyone, send out your best positive vibes.' He squeezed closer to Cathy for a better look at the screen. 'Any chance of that tea?' he added.

Andrew rolled his eyes and got up.

'Come on Cathy - we've got this.' Sammy's excitement was infectious and Cathy's fingers shook slightly as she typed her aunt's name into the search.

'Look for a mature lady in the images.'

'Yes okay I'm doing it,' said Cathy, clicking links.

'There! Look!' Sammy jabbed at the screen. 'She's old.'

Cathy frowned, 'yeah but I don't know what Karen looks like. This could be...'

Her heart stopped.

'What?' Sammy tried to snatch the laptop back. 'What have you seen?'

Andrew hurried back in. 'Wait wait, don't open anything yet.'

Cathy couldn't speak. She pointed at a photo of a stylish woman in huge dangly earrings and scarf draped effortlessly around her shoulders. Her wry smile into the camera was all knowing and kind.

'Is that her?' demanded Andrew.

Sammy read aloud the caption underneath.

Karen Douglas MBE

Cathia Design, Bath

'Well?'

'Uh...I think she's our Karen.' Cathy's chin wobbled. 'Vera told me she was into art and design. That might be her studio, her business or...something.' She tailed off, transfixed by the image in front of her.

Andy swung round. *'Cathia,'* he said, his eyes wide. 'That's you.'

Cathy's head dipped. The laptop screen blurred. 'My proper name, yes. Cathia Douglas.'

THIRTY-THREE

Google had opened the doors. *Cathia, Bath* was on Facebook, Instagram, Twitter - everywhere. Cathy devoured every scrap of information, glued to the computer until eventually even Sammy and Andrew drifted away, saying something about going to the pub.

Cathy's investigations told her *Cathia* was an art gallery in Bath city centre, which specialised in showcasing up and coming artists, graduates and new faces in the art world, old and young. Inclusivity was the order of the day, it seemed.

She hunted round for more details about Karen herself. There were very few photos but in each one, the same compassionate, wise eyes looked directly into the camera. A mix of confidence, worldliness and a no-nonsense attitude laced with kindness. Cathy burned to meet her.

When she finally looked up, the room had darkened around her. It was early evening and the autumn nights were closing in. Cathy worked her way around the Internet a little more, secured accommodation in Bath, texted Andrew with her plans, threw a few things into her case, organised a car and was on her way. She figured it would take between two and three hours to get there.

Driving at night suited her. Cathy listened to a podcast about contemporary British artists as she sped down the M4, effortlessly overtaking middle-laners who were dead set intent on hogging the road. She smiled at their lack of self-awareness, wound patiently through nighttime road works and enjoyed the experience of handling a fast, comfortable car. By the time she'd cleared the London lights, it had started to rain.

Bath opened up to her as she drove down wet streets to her hotel. Cathy glimpsed topiary trees in elegant planters down paved laneways. A lone bicycle was propped against a set of railings outside the Georgian facade of a terraced house. People hurried along the pavement sheltering under umbrellas. A sharp pop of laughter burst from a group of glamorous young people in well-cut suits and flowing ball gowns, dashing towards a waiting taxi.

The Jacobson was an imposing building of honey-coloured Bath stone and as Cathy drew up outside, a valet appeared from its glowing interior. Cathy hovered, feeling a little redundant as he retrieved her case from the boot and followed her inside. Richly decorated in red and bronze tones, the hotel foyer was an opulent cocoon and Cathy allowed herself to be organised by the efficient receptionist. He completed the paperwork and when Cathy politely turned down the offer of help with her luggage, explained the inner workings of the lift and gave directions to the room. Cathy nodded and smiled, now more than ready to fall into bed.

WHEN SHE AWOKE, Cathy's face was deep in a feather pillow. She lay there for a moment, relishing the stillness and then rolled onto her back with a sigh, opening her arms to the high ceiling. A thin line of light ran like a raindrop between heavy brocade drapes.

She picked up her phone and smiled at Andy's message of outrage at being excluded from the adventure. She felt a little conflicted, but Cathy knew she needed to see Karen for the first time by herself. She texted back a line of hearts and flowers and a promise to call later.

The reality of her situation was growing. She hadn't yet contacted *Cathia*, opting to turn up unannounced and scope things out. Perhaps a part of her wanted to delay the possibility of rejection. The gallery was only a few minutes' walk away.

Last night's rain had slowed to a misty drizzle and as she left the hotel, Cathy picked up the pace so by the time she found the gallery's street, she was breathless with exertion and apprehension. And then she was there, standing in front of a set of double doors with the gallery name etched into the glass. There was a board outside, presumably advertising current or forthcoming exhibitions, but Cathy didn't stop to read it. She walked up a couple of shallow steps and seized one of two tubular brass handles, pushed the door open and stepped inside.

She became aware of an inviting, light-filled space with white walls and an atmosphere of calm. A young woman with dark curly hair and green-framed spectacles looked up from behind a reception desk and smiled as Cathy approached, her boots echoing on the pale wooden floor.

'Good morning.'

Cathy's flittering heartbeat reverberated high in her chest.

'Hello.'

'Welcome to *Cathia*. My name's Violet. How may I help you?'

'Hi.' Cathy stopped. She hadn't thought beyond finding the place and now she was here, how on earth could she explain what she wanted? *I'd like to meet your boss. I think she holds the key to my life. Normally I'd take a tour of the gallery, but what I want right now are answers.*

Violet leaned over the counter and hooked a pamphlet from a stand.

'This is our current programme of events and exhibitions. Everything on the ground floor is free of charge and there is a nominal cost to our gallery space upstairs. The current exhibition is...'

'Is Karen Douglas here?' blurted Cathy, embarrassed that Violet had launched into her welcome speech when Cathy had no intention of looking at art.

The younger woman pulled up. She reddened slightly.

Cathy held up an apologetic hand. 'I'm sorry.' She settled

her shoulders. 'I'd like to see Karen if she's available please. Is she here?'

Violet looked at Cathy curiously, 'No, she doesn't come in every day. I can call the manager for you though.' She stretched out her hand for the phone.

'No, it's alright,' said Cathy hurriedly. She took a deep breath. 'Would you mind giving Karen a message for me? Look, I'll give you my number - perhaps she could call me.'

'What is it concerning?' Violet scanned a wide hallway to the left, as though willing another staff member to come to her aid.

Cathy hesitated. 'It's personal,' she said lamely and then, 'my name is Cathy Douglas. If you would just ask Karen to call me.'

Violet kept a neutral expression and slid a pad of paper and pen across the counter. 'Well jot down your details and I'll let her know you called by.'

'Thank you,' said Cathy scribbling her number on the pad. She felt Violet's interested stare. A mysterious American woman named Douglas turning up and asking to see Karen. Who could she be?

'Actually,' said Violet cutting across Cathy's thoughts, 'we have a couple of tickets still available for tonight's reception if you're interested.'

'Sorry?'

Violet came round the counter and handed her a flyer.

'Karen is holding a drinks reception tonight at The Great Bath.'

Cathy glanced at the paper in her hand. The headline read *Towards the Light.*

'This is a photographic competition, sponsored by Karen,' continued Violet, pointing at the pamphlet. 'It's an amazing opportunity for photography students to get their work noticed and the top three photos will be exhibited at *Cathia* in the New Year. Tonight's event is to celebrate the finalists and announce the winner. Bath's glitterati will be there - and what a venue.' She smiled encouragingly.

'Karen's hosting it?'

'Yeah, she does a lot of this kind of thing. I was thinking it would be a good opportunity for you to see her.' Violet watched Cathy's face. 'Are you okay?' she asked hesitantly. 'Do you need to sit down?'

Cathy drew in a breath. 'I'm fine,' she said as brightly as possible. 'Probably just hungry.'

'Ah - well may I recommend the Pump Room Restaurant?' said Violet, sounding relieved. 'It's at the Roman Bath site and a lovely spot for coffee and cake.'

'Sounds perfect.' Cathy looked again at the leaflet in her hand. 'And thank you for this, I'd love to go.' She opened her purse, to pay.

THIRTY-FOUR

Being at *Cathia* and inside Karen's world had thrown Cathy for a loop. She followed Violet's directions to the Pump Room, where almost immediately her frazzled nerves softened. Seated amid the splendour and history of the place, Cathy allowed the polite rise and fall of murmured conversations, the glittering chandelier and classical music to slow her bouncing heart and she finally got the jitters under control.

An hour later fortified by coffee and scones, she left the Pump Room feeling stronger - and to her immense relief, the claustrophobic feeling of panic from earlier at *Cathia* had gone. As she stepped out into a busy Bath morning, her phone rang and she moved aside to answer, sheltering under a shop awning of taut green canvas.

'Hi Andy.'

'Hey you! How's it going?'

'Good. I found the gallery; I found *Cathia*.'

He inhaled sharply. 'Was Karen there?'

'No, but listen, she's hosting a reception tonight at the Roman Baths and I've got a ticket.'

'Hey sis!' came a second voice.

Cathy smiled. 'Hi Sammy.'

'What's this thing you're going to?'

'It's a drinks reception for a photographic competition. Something to do with the university - I think Karen's a patron. Anyway, she'll be there. I left my number at the gallery too, so she may call.'

'Wow, how're you feeling?'

Cathy stared out at the crowds milling around the Baths, taking photos and listening to tour guides.

'A little nervous I guess, but mainly excited, now. It was very strange being at the gallery though - I wasn't prepared for that.'

'What are you gonna wear?' demanded Sammy. 'You can't go looking like something the cat dragged in - no offence. But Bath's got great shops. Get amongst it girl!'

She laughed. 'Okay boss.'

'Do you want us to drive down?' said Andrew earnestly, 'we can be there by tonight.'

'No, it's alright. Thanks though,' said Cathy, 'and Sammy I promise I'll buy something spectacular to wear.'

'Send a photo!'

'Ha, alright.' Suddenly she missed them both terribly. 'So I'll see you guys soon.'

'Good luck with everything,' said Andrew 'and take care. We love you.'

AFTER LUNCH, Cathy was back in her room at the Jacobson, trying on her new outfit - a classy, long-sleeved black jump suit with wide legs and a deep V-neck. She felt good, but her nerves were getting the better of her. She flicked through TV channels and tried to nap, but the afternoon dragged. Finally the day dwindled and she took herself off to the bathroom to get ready. It seemed very odd to Cathy to take a selfie in the mirror, but she'd promised Sammy so it had to be done.

A text bounced back.

OMG. You look fantastic. Love the statement earrings and red lippy!

And then Andy.

Good luck tonight. So proud to call you my sister. x

The nerves had come back. Cathy's heart thudded hard as she set off in the dark. It was a cold night and she regretted not buying a coat. Sammy had suggested a leather jacket; perhaps she should have listened. At least her funky gold clogs gave her a bit of height; their wooden heels clunked with each step, sounding far more confident than she felt.

As she approached the Roman Baths, Cathy checked her phone for the hundredth time, but there was still no message from Karen. She tried to control her shallow breathing, and shivered - whether from the cold or fearfulness she couldn't be sure. Her ticket was in her hand well before she arrived. She checked the time. And the venue. And the date.

The Great Bath took her breath away. Though outdoors, it was sheltered from the elements and the ethereal atmosphere unlike anything Cathy had experienced before. A smiling young couple were gathering tickets and Cathy mutely handed hers over, in awe of her magnificent surroundings and vaguely aware of people standing in well-dressed groups of two or three, while polished wait staff weaved through the throng with trays of champagne flutes. She accepted an offered glass and stood in front of the Great Bath itself, gazing at the deep green water and steam silently rising into the night air. Then, icy cold and delicious, the champagne fizzed on her lips and she snapped back in. A rush of voices and colour crowded her head and she realised she'd been standing trance-like, transfixed by the beauty of this mystical place.

'Cathia.'

She froze. She knew this voice. It had come to her in dreams and imaginings her whole life. It was the voice she'd longed to hear when her father had hit her, when her mother rejected her, when her brothers ignored her. She stared at the drink in her hand, astonished to see she was shaking.

Then a soft touch on her wrist. Enormous rings on slender fingers, the subtle clash of silver bangles. It took all Cathy's strength to lift her head, her mouth so dry she could barely speak.

'Hello Karen.'

'COME, LET'S TALK FOR A MOMENT.' Karen's voice was clear; refined. She touched Cathy's arm and steered her to one side.

'I'm sorry I didn't get a chance to call you today,' she added softly. 'Violet told me you'd be here, so I was hoping to catch you.'

Cathy's face burned in the October chill. Tremors spiraled through her body; she felt detached, clumsy.

'How'd you know who I was?'

'Oh Cathia, I'd know you anywhere.'

'Would you?'

She searched Karen's eyes and saw only kindness. Everything about her was understated - the expensively cut grey hair, smudge of pink on her lips, bold, modern jewelry. Nothing jarring, only quiet good taste. Cathy caught a few notes of her crisp light perfume. No old-lady lavender water and powder-puff scents for her.

'I'm sorry,' she mumbled, 'I don't think I'm ready for this. I shouldn't have come.'

'I'm so glad you did,' said Karen, 'thank you for finding me. Let's meet again tomorrow. Come to my home and we'll talk.'

Cathy had never felt so off-kilter and confused. This moment was actually happening. She'd achieved her goal of finding Karen. The impulse dash to Bath, showing up the gallery, agonising over the perfect outfit - everything had been leading up to this meeting. And now all she wanted to do was bolt for the door.

She caught sight of Violet hovering in her peripheral vision.

'I think you're wanted,' she said.

'Yes, it's time for my speech. Please stay for a while if

you'd like to. I have to be a dutiful host tonight and mingle with our guests, but may I just say, it's wonderful to see you. Truly. I'll text you my address and we can have some privacy tomorrow. Would that be alright?'

'Okay.'

Karen gently pressed her hand. 'Goodnight Cathia. I'll see you in the morning.'

Cathy wanted Karen to keep talking in her sweet measured voice, she wanted to gaze into her soft grey eyes, she wanted Karen's hand to keep holding hers, but already their fingers were slipping apart. *Don't go.*

She swallowed down a hard lump of tears.

'Goodnight.'

THIRTY-FIVE

She had to keep it together. Cathy turned her face away from the room and took deep breath after deep breath. Rattled and emotional, she struggled to stay calm, praying nobody would come over and speak with her.

The genial chitchat and discreet string quartet were interrupted by a faint whine of microphone feedback and then Violet's confident voice.

'Hello everyone. Good evening.'

The haunting, lofty space stilled, all eyes now focused on an area towards the back and away from the deep cool waters of the bath, where a small stage had been set up. Violet waited until she had the crowd's attention.

'On behalf of *Cathia Design*, I would like to welcome you all to The Great Bath, where we have gathered to celebrate three extraordinarily talented students and their wonderful photographs; the top three entries of this year's competition. And to announce the winner of this prestigious award please welcome *Cathia* founder and one of Bath's greatest supporters of the arts, Karen Douglas.'

From her spot in a shadowy corner, Cathy downed a slug of champagne and watched as a smiling Karen mounted two steps to the side of the stage and took the microphone, while the crowd clapped enthusiastically.

'Thank you Violet.'

Karen's quiet authority and confidence spoke volumes about her lifetime of living and working in a world she understood. Her relaxed demeanour so different from Cathy's, whose stomach was still in knots from their meeting.

'Before I announce the winner of this year's competition, I'd like to spend a moment or two on the work of each of the three finalists.'

She paused and Cathy noticed three large easels set up in semi-darkness to one side of the stage.

'Firstly,' said Karen, *'Tunnel of Love* by Simone Lewis.'

A spotlight came on above the first easel, where sat an enormous black and white photograph of two people perfectly framed by the railway tunnel they are walking through, towards a circle of light at the end.

A murmur of appreciation ran through the crowd and Cathy spotted a group of young people jostling and smiling at a pink-cheeked girl in their midst.

'And now,' said Karen when the noise had subsided, *'Tails of the Unexpected*, by Angus McFleet.' As a second spotlight shone down onto the next photo, a shift ran through the assembled guests. This picture was taken under the sea, looking up through layers of cobalt and turquoise water to blindingly bright sunshine. An intriguing shadow low down on the left and disappearing out of shot appeared to be a large fish tail - or could it be a mermaid? The photograph drew admiring glances towards a carefully scruffy young man, standing to one side with his arm around a titian-haired girl.

'Thank you,' said Karen to regain everyone's attention. 'And our third finalist is *First Light* by Maddy Fishbourne.'

The next spotlight revealed the final photo - a black and white shot taken vertically between two skyscrapers at dusk, with the brilliant white explosion of a streetlight coming on and intersecting the two buildings. There were nods of approval among the guests and Cathy picked up a few whispered comments about timing and capturing the artificial light so beautifully. She cast about for the photographer and spotted a petite student in denim overalls and boots amongst a gaggle of friends, clutching her glass of champagne as she dipped her head in acknowledgement of their support.

'Congratulations to all three of our finalists,' said Karen and the crowd broke into heartfelt applause. Cathy tapped her fingers against her champagne flute and couldn't take her eyes off Karen, holding the audience in the palm of her hand. She might be in her eighties but this woman was a powerhouse.

The room settled, waiting for her.

Karen ran a quick glance around the faces. Relaxed and unhurried, she took her time.

'Let's think for a moment about the theme for this year's competition. The brief for our students was *Towards the Light* and as you can see, each of our finalists has given careful thought to what this might mean and in particular, what it means to them.' She paused.

'What comes to mind when you hear that title?' Karen cocked her head slightly to one side, '*Towards the Light*. Could it mean you're coming from a place of darkness? Could it mean moving closer to an ending, or...' her gentle eyes found Cathy's, 'could it mean moving closer to a beginning?'

Dumbfounded, Cathy stood rooted to the spot. Karen was speaking directly and only to her.

'I like to think of it as moving closer to a brighter tomorrow,' she continued, 'to a place of healing and hope and sunshine.' Her features softened into the merest hint of a smile.

Cathy blinked and nibbled her bottom lip to stop it from quivering, but didn't waver or look away. And only when Karen turned again to the three huge canvases, did Cathy allow a single tear to fall.

IT WAS simple enough to slip away. Everyone's attention was on the stage and Cathy, already on the fringe of the proceedings, discreetly left her glass on a table and quietly walked out.

It was raining again. Cathy put her head down and marched resolutely in the direction of her hotel and once there, and safely in her room, opened the mini-bar and poured herself a glass of wine. For once she didn't care about or even take notice of, the vintage. She eased off her damp clogs and sat on the floor at the end of her king-sized bed to call Andy.

As soon as he answered, her throat closed up. She drew her knees into a-frame shapes and pressed the fingers of her free hand into her eye sockets.

'What happened?' Andrew's voice was full of concern.

Cathy shook her head into the phone. 'Nothing,' she whispered. 'Nothing bad, anyway.'

'Are you crying?'

She quivered slightly. 'Yeah.'

There was silence on the other end of the line. Gradually, Cathy pulled herself together. If Andy had pushed, she'd have simply hung up and then there would be endless rounds of apologising and explaining and all sorts of nonsense, but Andrew simply understood. He waited for her.

'Okay.' Cathy ran one hand over her face and sniffed. 'Here's the thing. It was actually fine. I met Karen and she was lovely, but I didn't expect my emotions to punch me in the guts like that. I know this is gonna sound bizarre, but I feel like Karen knows me already. She *gets* me, somehow. It's weird and a little scary, but also incredible and beautiful at the same time. God, I wish I smoked, I'd be sucking on one of Vera's ciggies by now.' She laughed weakly.

'Are you alone?'

'Yeah I'm at the hotel.' She paused. 'You're not worried about me are you?'

'You sound a bit strung out,' said Andrew, 'and I still don't know what happened tonight.'

'I will tell you in every detail when I get back, I promise. I'm going to see Karen again tomorrow at her home and I'll be better prepared this time. Tonight it was really brief because she was hosting the event and had to get up on stage and speak, but even in the few moments we had together, I felt something...a real connection. And then when she was talking about the photographs and the theme, she looked across the room and it felt like she was talking straight at me...I don't know Andy, it was surreal. It pulled me apart.'

'Shit Cathy, I wish you weren't by yourself. You've got all these unanswered questions...'

'Yep. A mile long and I can't think of a single one right now.'

'God,' he muttered, 'this isn't right.'

She pictured his face crisscrossed with worry and felt a huge swell of love. It made her strong.

'I don't want you stressing about me. I'm really alright - it's just, you know, a lot. I'm so glad I came here though and can't wait for tomorrow. Do not worry - you hear?'

A smile trickled through. 'Okay.'

'Hey,' said Cathy, 'where's Sammy?'

'Rehearsals, but I'm going to meet him at the theatre bar later.'

'Give him a hug from me.'

'Will do.'

'G'night then.'
'Night, sis.'
'Andy?'
'Yeah?'
'Thanks.'

THIRTY-SIX

A short walk from the city centre, Karen's apartment complex was tucked away in a private park. A well-watered green lawn was set amid a quadrangle of mellow terraces, with a short flight of steps leading to each apartment. Cathy stood in the middle of the grassed area and rotated in a slow circle, admiring the clever way old and new had melded, where listed building seamlessly met new construction.

She found Karen's number neatly displayed on a small plaque set into the wall, and mounted the steps to her front door. The surrounding trees shivered and sighed in the breeze. A faint hum of traffic played like a soundtrack in the distance. Something inside her stirred; the place was perfect for Karen and this pleased Cathy enormously, though she didn't know why. The roiling emotions of the previous night had simmered down and peacefulness washed through her in soft waves. She'd felt stuck with pins with one revelation after another ever since the email from Eric's solicitor in Guildford, and she'd found herself bracing for shock after shock. When Karen had spoken to her from the stage last night, it all came to a head and while Cathy shoved everything to one side as best she could to get through those moments, the second Andy hung up, she'd put her forehead on her knees and sobbed. She wept for her childhood, for being lied to and abused, for not knowing who she was or to whom she belonged. Cathy's entire sense of self had been knocked down and still she didn't know how she'd come to be born. It wasn't out of love, she was sure of that; her mother had all but told her so and Edward clearly despised her. She thought about the main players in the story of her life - gentle Eric, passionate Vera, arrogant Edward, long-suffering Dot and the ethereal Karen, but with each new discovery, they revealed themselves as horses of very different colours; Eric seemed ineffectual and weak, Vera, selfish and weak, Edward cruel and weak, and Dot, scheming and weak. But what about Karen?

She knocked on the door.

'GOOD MORNING CATHIA.'

Karen looked a little tired around the eyes, but her smile was as warm and genuine as the night before.

'Come in,' she said stepping back into a hallway of grey and white stone tiles.

Cathy hesitated, wondering if it would be appropriate to give Karen a kiss on the cheek. She waited a fraction too long and then leaned in, clumsily knocking against Karen's jaw.

If she noticed the fumbled show of affection, Karen didn't let on. Instead she briefly held Cathy's upper arm and accepted the kiss on the side of her face as though it were completely normal.

Embarrassed, Cathy trailed along behind as Karen made for the generously proportioned staircase.

'This way,' she said over her shoulder.

Upstairs was a spacious apartment, where hardwood sash windows offered stunning views over the city. The place was beautifully curated, calm and dressed in soft tones. A haven.

'Wow,' said Cathy as Karen made for the kitchen 'you have the most incredible art.' She stopped in front of a huge abstract painting in various shades of grey with a dramatic splash of blue and white in one corner.

'Thank you. I've been a collector for many years and all these pieces have a story. Tea?'

'I'd love one.'

'Please - sit.'

Cathy slipped onto a beechwood stool at a large marble-topped island and slid her bag onto the floor at her feet.

'You have a beautiful home,' she said. 'Have you lived here long?'

Karen retrieved cups and saucers from a cupboard above the sink. 'I've been in Bath for a very long time, and bought this place - let me see, probably about ten years ago now.'

Cathy watched her small capable hands as they went

through the ritual of tea making. This lady might be in the twilight of her life, her hair might be grey and her skin a little wrinkled, but she had the bearing of a much younger woman. She carried a tray of tea and biscuits over to the island where Cathy sat, watching her.

'And you're in the Napa Valley,' said Karen matter-of-factly.

Cathy's brow crinkled. 'How do you know?'

Karen poured the tea.

'Sorry,' said Cathy, 'that came out wrong. I didn't mean to sound rude.'

'You're not rude, Cathia. It's a perfectly acceptable question.'

'Did Vera tell you?'

Karen stopped. Her hands fell into her lap. 'Dear, dear Vera. How is she these days?'

'You're not in touch?'

'No. But I've tried to keep up with all your adventures in the States.'

'Have you?'

'Yes. The Internet is quite wonderful.' Karen twinkled at her.

'Hold on - you've face-stalked me?'

'Is that what they call it? How funny.'

Cathy held her gaze. 'Look I have to say, you don't seem surprised I'm here. And to be honest with you, it's freaking me out a bit that I'm sitting in your kitchen having a cup of tea, like it's nothing.'

'It feels so right to me,' said Karen softly. 'It's all I've ever wanted.'

'I don't understand.' Cathy could feel a tightness in her chest. It was as though she was the only one not in on the joke. Was it a joke to Karen? Was *she* a joke?

'I want to tell you everything. I'm an old lady now, Cathia and who knows how much time I have left? I cannot begin to express how much I've longed to see you; be near you. And if I seem lukewarm about our meeting now, please forgive me because complacency is the last thing I feel. I've spent my life being so careful about showing my true emotions. I had no one but myself to lean on. There have been very few people I've trusted and I learned that in order to get any semblance of happiness, I need to be completely independent.'

'Your husband cheated,' said Cathy sharply. 'No wonder you don't trust people.'

Karen's head tipped slightly to one side.

'Eric was a good man.'

'Who cheated on you.'

'It wasn't like that, Cathia.'

'Yes, so Vera says. Apparently you were in on the whole thing.'

The atmosphere cooled.

Cathy's lips formed a hard line. She felt upset and confused and knew she was snapping.

Unruffled, Karen regarded her and gently cleared her throat.

'May I try to explain?'

Cathy gave a terse nod. She must not cry.

'Alright.' Karen stopped. 'Cathia, it's important to remember this was the 1960s. Times were different. I was married to Eric, yes...'

My father, apparently,' interrupted Cathy.

'I was married to Eric,' continued Karen smoothly 'and we loved one another very much. We truly did. We wanted a baby but I couldn't conceive. And when I say we wanted a baby, Eric wanted a child, but I desperately needed to be a mother. I felt like I was born to bear children and when I couldn't, it broke me.'

'I know what that's like.'

'What?' Karen's poise slipped a little.

'I'm childless, but not through choice. I *couldn't* have babies.'

'Like me,' said Karen in a small voice.

'Yes.'

'Cathia, I'm so sorry. I didn't know.'

'Well how could you?'

Karen gave a slow shake of her head.

'Please,' said Cathy after a pause, 'I need to know your story, because it's also my story and nobody will tell me what it is.'

'As I said before, I longed to be a mother. I loved Eric and I know he loved me, but we couldn't have a family. Vera and Edward, on the other hand, could. They had Mark and Paul of course.'

Cathy nodded, her pulse slowly settling as she concentrated on Karen's voice.

'Lawrence and Barbara Hasting arrived on the scene from America.'

'I know them. I was married to Junior - did you know?'

Puzzled, Karen looked up. 'When?'

'Years ago. The 1980s,' Cathy sighed, 'it didn't last.'

'What happened?'

Cathy smiled sadly. 'Well, as we've already established, I couldn't have babies.'

Neither of them spoke for a moment.

'Go on with the story,' mumbled Cathy eventually, 'the Hastings?'

'Yes, said Karen. 'Vera and I were put in charge of entertaining Barbara while she was in London with Larry, while the men - Eric and Edward - worked on securing the advertising account. It was always our job to keep the wives amused back then and we didn't mind - Vera and I were so close and we had a lot of fun. Anyway, we became really quite pally with Barb. She's a lovely woman.'

'Yes,' said Cathy quickly, 'she was so kind to me. There was nothing she could do to save my marriage, but I felt I had a great ally in my mother in law.'

Karen nodded. 'So Vera, Barb and I became this little trio and I ended up confiding in her. She told us about a concept she'd heard of in America, which I now know as surrogacy. Of course, it wasn't known about in the 1960s. I believe it wasn't seen as a viable option until the 1970s although it's been going on forever really and often amongst family members.'

Cathy's eyes widened. 'Barbara said the four of you should get together to make a baby?'

'Not exactly. And let me tell you, it wasn't an easy decision by any means. We girls were horrified when Barb suggested it and then Eric was appalled when we finally told him and Edward - well - he hit the roof.' Karen gave a sorrowful shake of her head. 'Poor Vera.'

'But you went ahead with it anyway?' Cathy leaned closer.

'We did. It was the hardest, most upsetting thing in the world. Believe me, I hated knowing what was going on between Eric and Vera, but the ache of childlessness was worse, so I sort of shut my eyes to it all.'

'Vera said something about you being present during...it...and it was like a threesome.' Cathy gave an involuntary shudder.

'Cathia, please believe me, it wasn't like that. Your father simply couldn't do it. He loved me and didn't want to hurt me so when he and Vera tried...'

'He wanted you there, too.' Cathy stopped. 'That's kind of creepy and weird.'

Karen gave a delicate cough. 'I left the room for the actual...'

'Oh. God. Alright. Yes, I see.' Cathy bit her lip, not wanting to hear more, yet wanting to hear everything.'

'And,' continued Karen, 'Vera became pregnant.'

'With me,' said Cathy flatly.

'Yes.'

Cathy pondered this for a moment 'Why then did I end up

with Vera and Edward? Did you and Eric change your minds about having a baby?'

'God, no.' Karen's eyes grew wide. 'No, definitely not. Cathia, it was a terrible, terrible time. Vera planned to look after the baby - you - for your first few months and all the while she would be working towards leaving Edward for good.'

'Wait. So Edward didn't know I was Eric's child?'

'He found out.'

'How?'

Karen hesitated.

'Vera told him?'

Karen's face was rigid with pain. 'She didn't mean to.'

Cathy took it in, her mind running wildly.

'She got drunk?'

'I think so, yes. There was a massive row. Edward discovered her housekeeping money saved up and it all came out. He...' She stopped. 'He pounded your mother to a pulp. Vera ended up in the hospital; a fractured jaw, split lip, swollen eyes...he punched her *so hard*. And then he started kicking...' Karen covered her face with her hands, '...and...and she couldn't have any more babies after that. And Vera lied and lied to everyone - all the doctors and nurses, everyone. She was so frightened of Edward. He threatened...'

Cathy gasped. 'To kill her?'

Karen slowly lowered her hands, tears streaming down her cheeks. 'Worse - he threatened to kill her children.'

'Jesus.'

'And he would have, you know. He was like a wild

animal - terrifying and unpredictable. His cold cold rage. What could she do?'

Hatred for Edward bolted through Cathy like a knife. She stared across the room and through the kitchen window to the city in the distance. Everything she was being told whirled around and around her head until she became aware of Karen, softly weeping. Cathy reached for her. There were no words.

THIRTY-SEVEN

They went for a walk in the woodland grounds of Karen's apartment complex. Arm in arm, they skirted wet drifts of shiny golden leaves heaped under the twisting branches of ancient trees, and talked about the past.

'Why did you leave The Narrows?' asked Cathy when they stopped to rest on a bench overlooking the valley.

Karen gazed into the middle distance.

'My marriage to Eric couldn't survive. The strain was unbearable - knowing you were there, only a few doors down from our house and yet we couldn't see you.'

'Edward banned you?'

'Indeed. Vera tried every trick in the book, but Edward always found out. I think he made Mark and Paul his little spies and bless their hearts, they were so scared of him they did his bidding. And every time, Vera would bear the brunt of his temper. Before you were six months old he'd broken her nose twice and goodness knows how many times her ribs were smashed.'

'What did he want?'

'He wanted her to pay for what she'd done.'

'Which was what, exactly? Her intentions were good - she was only trying to help, wasn't she?'

'Oh, Edward didn't see it like that. It was betrayal of the very worst kind, not only by his most prized possession, his beautiful wife, but his twin brother, too.'

'Yes, what about Eric? It sounds like all Edward's rage was directed at Vera.'

'He never spoke to his twin again. Can you imagine? Eric was heartbroken, he really thought Edward would understand in time, but he never did.'

'It's a hard thing though,' said Cathy thoughtfully, 'to know the two people closest to you in the world, would go behind your back like that. I suppose in his eyes it was the ultimate act of treachery.'

'He did know about it,' replied Karen, 'and Vera was severely punished, but he'd already lost her by that point. She longed to leave, but had no means of supporting herself or her children.'

'Well then how could she possibly expect to divorce Edward once the baby was born?'

Karen sighed. 'We were so young, so naive and we clung to any solution, no matter how flimsy. Vera convinced herself she could make the break after a few months. We would have helped her financially as much as we could but she was determined to leave Edward, come what may.'

Cathy rubbed her temple, grappling with the strands of the story. 'It *was* naive, given how cruel and controlling her husband was.'

'Actually,' said Karen, 'I think it was courageous. It takes real guts to stand up to a powerful bully like Edward and remember, this is 1966. Women really didn't have much of a voice and Vera had no independence. It was an unrealistic dream - yes perhaps, but at least Vera had one.'

Silence fell. And then.

'Did you and Eric know about the abuse Vera suffered?'

Karen stared down at her gloved hands.

'Not for a long time. Years. They both hid it so well; you would have thought them the perfect couple.'

'And yet you and Vera were best friends.'

Karen regarded her through pale, watery eyes.

'Yes. And I've lived with the guilt of overlooking the signs ever since. What kind of friend was I? Too selfish and focused on my own problems to see what was right in front of me. I failed her; my beautiful, brave Vera.'

Cathy sat back, as images of her mother flashed through her mind. The shame she'd felt as a child when Vera would turn up at school with smeared make-up and unruly hair, tottering on stilettos as she grabbed Cathy's chubby hand and stumbled home. And once there, she'd fall on the couch with a lit cigarette, cradling a bottle, as Cathy and her brothers crept round the kitchen rifling through cupboards for something to eat while their mother snored off her hangover. And all too soon would come the terrifying sound of a key in the front door, sending all three kids skedaddling out of sight.

Even a pillow jammed over Cathy's head couldn't drown out the sounds of the row that would follow. The shouting and crashing sounds of two people so trapped in misery and hate, there was no room for love, not even for their children.

'How is she?'

Cathy came back to the present with a jolt.

'Vera? To tell you the truth, I don't really know.'

'She's drinking?'

'I'm afraid that's never going to change.'

'Is she happy?'

Cathy raised her shoulders. 'It's hard to tell. She's feisty though - does that count?'

Karen smiled weakly. 'Good to hear.' She paused. 'How is she physically?'

'Fine I think, though she has dementia.'

'Ah.' Karen's head dropped.

Cathy turned to her. 'Would you like to visit? We could go - I'll take you if you like.'

Karen hesitated. 'I'd love to see her, but do you think it's wise? I wouldn't want to make matters worse.'

'Oh Karen, how can they be worse?' Cathy gave a rueful half-laugh.

'I don't know if she's forgiven me.'

'For leaving?'

'For all of it. If it wasn't for me, she might still be married to Edward; her sons might still be in her life.'

'She was already an alcoholic though, wasn't she? And already a victim of Edward's abuse?'

'True.'

Cathy watched Karen's face intently. 'Have you forgiven her?'

'Oh, I grappled so hard with that. It took me a long, long time to accept I was never going to be your mother. For years I hated them all; Vera, Edward - even poor Eric. And, not surprisingly, the person I hated most of all was myself. My descent into darkness was rapid and extreme. I'd lost you before I even had you and my despair nearly killed me. I couldn't bear to be so close and yet excluded from your life and I'm afraid I made some very poor decisions. I was a complete and utter mess and blamed Vera for not following through with her plan - though deep down I knew it was hopeless from the get-go. And yes, I forgave her eventually - she really had all her choices taken away and now here we are; two vulnerable old ladies, clinging to what's left of our lives, with all those years of shattered dreams behind us.'

'But Karen, you've led a remarkable life,' cried Cathy, 'look what you've done, what you've achieved.'

Karen's eyes were as full as the ocean.

'I had to do something, Cathia. I couldn't stay in that pit of hopelessness and somehow, *somehow* I dragged myself out. But what is it all for, really? What does anything actually mean? Things are nice, money is nice, achievements and acco-lades are nice, but darling, I didn't have you. So what did I do? I did the only thing I could - I tried and tried - so hard to make you proud.'

'Me? But...'

'I knew you'd find me. One day, I knew you'd find me. And look - now you're here. I couldn't chase after you, it wouldn't be fair, but I knew in my soul you would somehow feel our bond. You are the baby I so desperately wanted and I've loved you for the whole of your life.'

Cathy stared at her, stunned.

'I did feel a connection,' she murmured. 'I think I've been searching for you forever and I didn't understand why my life made no sense, why all my relationships failed. And when we finally met, it knocked me for six.'

'Oh, Cathia.'

Cathy shifted slightly. 'You always use my full name; you're the only person who does.'

Karen fished a tissue from her bag and composed herself. 'Vera let me choose your name; it was the one thing I was allowed to do. Edward never knew of course, but it's true.'

'But why *Cathia*?'

Karen gave a soft gasp. 'Oh my goodness, to hear you say you name...it's...'

A long moment passed and then another, while she struggled to keep herself in check. Finally she raised her chin.

'You were the one good thing to come out of this whole unspeakable mess, my darling. A precious little girl who should have been so cherished.'

She wiped away a solitary tear trickling slowly down Cathy's cheek.

'...and *Cathia* means pure.'

THIRTY-EIGHT

They went to see Vera.

All the way to Tunbridge Wells, Cathy convinced herself it was better to simply arrive with Karen rather than let Vera know in advance. She had no idea what her reaction would be, but as Karen had said, they were both old women now. Cathy had to agree there seemed no point in putting things off and if the meeting went badly, well so be it. She just hoped Vera would be sober.

'Goodness,' exclaimed Karen as they drew up at Honeysuckle Lodge, 'what a handsome house. This is lovely.'

Cathy felt a rush of pleasure that Karen cared about Vera's surroundings. How wonderful it would be for them to rekindle their friendship after fifty three years. She couldn't help but feel responsible for being the reason their relationship failed.

'I texted Andrew earlier,' she said as they made their way to the front door. 'I'd love you to meet him.'

Karen halted. 'Eric's son.'

'Andy's wonderful,' added Cathy quickly, 'and he can't wait to meet you - he and his partner helped me find you and they've been incredibly supportive through this whole thing. And Karen, remember he's my half-brother.'

'Heavens, of course he is,' said Karen with a low chuckle. 'My goodness Cathia, you've gained so much more than an inheritance, haven't you?'

'More than I ever could have imagined. I feel so blessed.' A little thrill darted through her. Finally she was bringing her family together.

They signed in and Cathy noticed the slight tremor in her hand as she wrote her name in full for the first time. Cathia Douglas. It felt so good.

A passing member of staff let them know Vera was in her room. Cathy gave a light tap and pushed against the partly closed door, which swung open to reveal her mother sitting in her easy chair by the window, reading the novel they'd bought in Tunbridge Wells. Cathy ran an automatic glance round the room, relieved to see nothing incriminating. A light breeze moved gently through the curtains; somebody had been in to make the bed and freshen the place up. Vera's handbag was safely out of reach. Cathy exhaled.

Karen was right behind her. Cathy sensed her calming presence; if she was nervous about this meeting she certainly didn't show it and Cathy took courage from that.

'Hi,' she said brightly, stepping into the room.

Vera raised her head and instantly her eyes moved past her daughter's face to the figure at Cathy's shoulder. Her forehead creased; she lowered the book to her lap.

'Hello Vera,' said Karen in her soft measured voice. She walked over to the window, a small smile hesitating around her mouth.

Vera shot a look at Cathy, loaded with something she couldn't interpret. She felt the blood rush to her face, suddenly panicked. Why hadn't she given Vera due warning of this visit? Her mother's unpredictability meant this could go either way.

Karen leaned in to kiss Vera's cheek and placed a small bouquet of white flowers across her knees. Vera's hand floated to Karen's shoulder and Cathy watched a river of tears flow through her eyes.

'Oh my God,' murmured Vera. Her voice sounded strangled, like it hurt to speak. 'Karen.'

Cathy jolted out of her reverie and dashed forward to drag the second chair close to Vera's and the two ladies' hands were linked as Karen lowered herself to the seat. They stared at one another without words, their gnarled jewelled fingers intertwining.

Then, as Cathy watched from her spot on the bed, Karen spoke.

'How are you, darling?'

Vera's chin dipped.

'Not so good.'

'No?'

'They tell me I'm sick. I can't seem to recall things very

well. I get muddled.'

'You remember me though, don't you?'

The pent-up tears spilled over. 'Oh God Karen, of course I do.'

Karen lightly squeezed her hands. 'I'm glad.'

Innate good manners came to the fore and Vera valiantly pulled herself together.

'And you?'

A small smile. 'I'm fine, dear.'

'I do hear bits and pieces you know,' said Vera, 'things in the paper - my famous sister in law.'

'Ah.' It was Karen's turn to drop her head. 'That's nice of you.'

'I've missed you,' blurted Vera, anguish filling her face.

Karen closed her eyes against a swelling tide. 'Me too, my splendid girl. Me too.'

Cathy watched with a thumping heart from across the room. She had no idea what to do and in the end, did nothing.

She wasn't needed here.

THIRTY-NINE

Karen was quiet on the drive up to Soho, later. Cathy kept giving little sideways glances as she drove, worried the visit might have upset her.

'Are you okay?'

Karen looked older, her cheeks a little hollow, her eyes a little bloodshot.

'I'm tired,' she replied, 'that's all.'

Cathy let a pause fall.

After a moment, Karen spoke again.

'It was so good to see Vera. Thank you for taking me, Cathia.'

'I wish I'd known you two back in the day.'

'My dear, we were invincible.'

'Ha. I bet.'

Karen leaned back against the headrest.

'Your mother was the prettiest girl in town. Super stylish,

and wicked fun. I loved her so much; still do. The sixties were the best; the fashion, art, music...it was an era of real optimism. So different from what had come before.'

'It wasn't all good though, was it?' said Cathy soberly. 'So many things went on behind closed doors. *What will the neighbours think?* and all that.'

Karen sighed. 'Indeed. Edward and Vera's marriage was a case in point.'

'A sham, really.'

'Sad to say, it's just the way it was. Not knowing - or not *seeing* what was actually going on, haunts me to this day.'

'What could you have done about it though?'

'At the very least, I could have let Vera know she wasn't alone.'

'Edward's an asshole,' muttered Cathy.

'I agree,' said Karen, 'a charming, gregarious, creative, handsome...asshole.'

'Who's not my father!' added Cathy brightly.

They both smiled.

'Do you blame Edward for Vera's self-destructive behaviour?' said Cathy.

'To be fair I'd have to say we all drank and smoked and partied.'

'Other drugs too?'

'Strangely, no. Not for us at any rate. Who knows what Edward was doing?'

'Well, quite.'

They drove for a couple of minutes without speaking.

'Would you rather I take you home tonight?' said Cathy,

breaking into their companionable silence. 'Andy will understand.'

Karen stirred. 'No, I'd like to stay in London and meet the boys,' she said. 'I'll rest my eyes for a while and then I'll be raring to go again.'

'Put your seat back,' said Cathy kindly. 'I'll give you a nudge when we get there.'

THEY'D ARRANGED to meet at Cathy's new favourite dining destination - the precinct near Andy's flat. November was fast approaching, bringing dank misty drizzle and low-lying skies. The air was hard and iron-cold.

Karen had perked up considerably by the time they arrived, applying fresh lipstick and giving her wrists a quick squirt of perfume before getting out of the car.

'I'm ready for a bite to eat now,' she declared. 'Maybe a glass of wine, too!'

Cathy gave her a hug. 'You're a real trooper, you know? Let's go.'

Cathy spotted Andrew and Sammy already seated at the table. When he saw them, Andy leapt up and hurried through the restaurant with his arms open.

'Cathy!' He gathered her up in a huge embrace and then turned to Karen. Politely, she held out her hand but Andy was having none of it and scooped her into his arms, too.

'It's so nice to meet you!'

Sammy arrived on the scene. 'Hello ladies,' he cried and

planted a kiss on both Karen's cheeks, then threw his arm around Cathy's shoulders.

'Come on,' he exclaimed, 'we've got the best table. I know the restaurant owner, he went to college with...doesn't matter...and we've got bubbly on the way - and oysters! We ordered oysters, didn't we Andy?'

'Yep, sure did.' Andrew guided everyone back to the table and Cathy caught Karen's eye as Sammy popped the champagne cork with a whoop, sending it ricocheting to the ceiling. They shared a smile and Cathy's heart filled up.

'Cheers!'

They all clinked their champagne flutes together and there was a pause while they took a sip.

'Well,' said Andy, 'how did it go at Honeysuckle Lodge?'

Karen put down her glass. 'It was wonderful to see Vera.' Her eyes shone in the warm restaurant lights. 'I'm so thankful to Cathia for taking me.'

'Will you visit her again?'

'I'd like to and maybe one day we could arrange for her to come to Bath.'

'That's a lovely idea,' said Cathy, 'let's see if we can sort something out before Christmas.'

'You're sticking around for a while?' said Andy, 'that's great!'

'Mmm.' Cathy ran a soft glance around the table. 'I've given it a lot of thought...oh man, I'm getting teary.' She cleared her throat. 'Okay, here's the thing. Everyone I love is right here in England. Everyone. I don't think I can bear to go away again; America really has nothing for me, any more.'

Andrew's eyebrows shot up. 'You're not going back?'

Cathy gave a little smile. 'There is one thing I'd like to do before leaving my life in America for good,' she said thoughtfully.' She looked straight into Karen's eyes. 'How would you feel about coming with me? Help me pack up? Wouldn't it be fun to go to California; check out the vineyards, have a little holiday? And while we're at it, let's put the gang back together; you and Vera and Barb.'

Karen gave a little gasp. 'Cathia! I would simply adore that.'

'Oh yay!' cried Sammy, 'can we come too?'

Cathy looked at Andrew. 'How about it, then?'

'Yes!' he declared, 'a thousand times yes. The Douglas family on tour. Somebody, please write a book about it.'

Cathy clapped her hands. 'You're on!'

'Now then,' said Sammy, 'before we go any further, I have one very important question.'

'Yes?' said Cathy, surprised by his serious tone.

Sammy let a dramatic pause fall.

'Who won the photography competition?' he said with his irrepressible grin.

Cathy let out a breath. 'Yes! I'd forgotten about that.'

Everyone looked at Karen.

She put her glass down. *Tunnel of Love,'* she said simply.

Cathy took a sharp breath. 'No way. I thought it would be *Tails of the Unexpected.* Those colours were so beautiful and the mysterious fin or tail or whatever it was, disappearing in the watery depths...'

Karen nodded. 'Yes, a stunning shot.'

'Or *First Light*,' continued Cathy. 'I loved how that photo was taken at dusk and first light referred to the street light.'

'I wish I'd seen them,' murmured Andy, 'they sound amazing.'

'They are all excellent,' said Karen, 'but *Tunnel of Love* came out on top.'

'Because it was the most technically difficult?' asked Sammy.

'Yes,' said Karen, 'capturing the light so perfectly would have been a real challenge, so in that respect, it was felt this was the best shot.'

'Ah,' said Andy, 'makes sense seeing as the theme was to do with light.'

Cathy watched them over the rim of her glass. She thought about the winning photo, about the people in the darkness walking towards the bright circle at the end. And she thought about what Karen had said from the stage that night at the Baths.

'Is the technical aspect the only reason you chose *Tunnel of Love?*' she said quietly.

'Hmmm.' Karen's voice was soft as velvet. 'Darling girl, how well you know me. The photo won on merit, but it has a little something extra that couldn't be ignored.'

'Which is?'

'It's love, Cathia. Love always wins, in the end.'

ACKNOWLEDGMENTS

First of all, I'd like to thank my mum and dad for having me in 1959, which meant I was alive and kicking in that astonishing decade, the sixties.

My wonderful brother was a teenager then and brought the 1960s youth culture into our family home, so I grew up hearing the music, taking in the fashions from the sidelines and soaking up that daring 'we can do anything' atmosphere. Writing The Narrows took me back to my childhood in Surrey, England and I loved all the little memories that sparked up through my research.

Huge thanks to Hammer and Tongs for producing the beautiful book I hold in my hands today and of course, a big thank you to the brilliant team at m. Media for bringing the cover of The Narrows to life. My heartfelt thanks also to booklovers and devourers of stories everywhere. What would we writers do without our readers?

And my beautiful family. You guys are my world. Thank you, team. x

www.ingramcontent.com/pod-product-compliance
Lightning Source LLC
Chambersburg PA
CBHW020634260626
47157CB00008B/2731